DRAGON WANTED

A CURVY GIRL DRAGON SHIFTER ROMANCE

MICHELLE ZIEGLER

INTRODUCTION

Do bad things always come in three?

First, a sinfully hot guy asks for her help. All Aisha needed to do was find an antidote, and she failed. Then, the grant she needed was denied.

Now her walking fantasy is back, but he doesn't want or need anything, except her. Little curvy, doesn't-fit-in, geeky her.

How does she say no when her soul wants him, but her head is torn between promises made and her heart?

She doesn't know, and she isn't sure what she'd risk to find out.

The next book in the Space Dragons Seek Mates series. Deo's story.

Copyright © 2020 Michelle Ziegler

All rights reserved. No part of this publication may be reproduced, distributed, or transmitted in any form or by any means, including photocopying, recording, or other electronic or mechanical method, without the prior written permission of the publisher, except in the case of brief quotations embodied in critical reviews and certain other noncommercial users permitted by copyright law. For permission requests, write to the publisher addressed "Attention: Permission coordinator," at the address below.
michelle@michellezieglerauthor.com

Publisher's Note: This is a work of fiction. Names, character, places, and incidents are a product of the author's imagination. Locales and public names are sometimes used for atmospheric purposes. Any resemblance to actual people, living, or dead, or to businesses, companies, events, institutions, or locales is completely coincidental.

You need to love you first.

ACKNOWLEDGMENTS

Life isn't easy. We are all different and those differences make us who we are. I should tell the world thank you for being you, because you inspire characters to be who they are.

My husband and kids always deserve my biggest thanks for letting me have time to get these characters out into the world!

I have so many readers to thank, but especially my Beta/Alpha readers. Thanks Lucia, Bev, Carol, and Donise! They have a knack for reading between the lines.

Thank you Emcat Designs for my cover and Editing by Elizabeth for services.

Of course, my review team is a group that has my undying gratitude!

AND ALWAYS! Thank you readers! Thank you for giving me a chance and escaping into my world and loving some confused dragon shifters from outer space. Thank you for following me this far into this crazy adventure.

*A*isha gripped the edge of the counter. She needed a cold shower. If Deo showed up one more time, she'd probably jump him.

Doing a favor for a hot guy seemed reasonable. Doing a favor for a man like him though, one that saw her, like really saw her, was not the plan.

God, when he looked at her. Aisha nearly moaned as a heat settled between her legs. Well, hell. This wasn't in her plan. He wasn't in her plan.

She gripped the counter harder, her knuckles starting to ache. She wasn't supposed to want him, though. Closing her eyes, she allowed herself a few more moments of living in a world that wasn't hers. What would it be like to be the woman that Deo wanted? To be the woman that earned his gazes of pure adoration. Hell, what would it be like just to be kissed by him?

"Aisha? Are you okay?"

Her eyes flew open as she swung around.

"I, yeah. Hi, Tan. I'm fine. Just super. Why do you ask?"

He shook his head as he walked in. "I dunno. You seemed to be having a moment with the table, I didn't want to disturb you."

Her face heated.

"You sure you're okay?" he asked, his eyes narrowed.

"Yeah. Fine. I was just thinking. My request for a grant was denied. Again."

What she really wanted to say was that she was tired of looking at life through a microscope. Both figuratively and literally. Deo, though. He was bigger than life. Both in size and that bulge in his pants. God, she struggled to keep her eyes on his face. For the first time in her life, she understood why men struggled to watch a woman's face. Aisha wasn't about to say anything, though.

If Tanmay filled out his pants like Deo, maybe they wouldn't be in this strange standstill in life. No, yeah. They still would. She just couldn't love him, not like she should.

Swallowing, Aisha realized that she was getting closer and closer to needing to have a conversation that she dreaded. Tan was a good man. But he wasn't right for her.

"You sure that's all that's going through your head?" he asked.

Aisha nodded. "Yeah. Sure. I mean, when isn't there science-y stuff going on in my head."

That got her an odd sideways glare. "Science-y? That's not a word."

She wrinkled her nose. Damn, she just sucked at relationships.

How did you tell the man your father arranged a marriage with that you were horny and having daydreams about another man? Hell, she still hadn't come up with a good way to break off the engagement. Maybe that little tidbit would end it?

Lucky for her, or maybe unlucky, Tan didn't exactly seem to pick up on any of this. They'd sort of fallen into a happy coexistence. One where there was suitable conversation, sometimes a laugh or two, and zero sexual chemistry. He'd filled some voids.

Moving to her test tubes, she plucked one from the stand and shook it up.

What the hell was even in this one?

"You're acting a little odd, Aisha," said Tan.

Blowing out a breath, she glared. "I'm a chubby female scientist with permanent bags under my eyes. What exactly screams normal here?"

His picture-perfect smile should have done something for her. Then she thought of Deo and her entire body heated. No. Something was super wrong with her.

"True. But you're still acting oddly. Maybe you have a fever?" he asked.

Oh crap. Did she? Her hand flew to her forehead. Nope. Well, maybe. It was a Deo fever, and she needed to stop it. Cold shower. Only, in the lab, all she had was the safety mandated shower and eyewash station. Well, maybe that would work.

"I'm fine. Really. It's just been a crap day. I was depending on that grant. Maybe I just need to face the fact I'm still nowhere, like the rest of the world."

Focusing on her failure cooled down her libido a bit. She wasn't able to help Deo, and now she was letting down the rest of the world.

"It's okay, Aisha. Millions of people are trying to cure cancer. You've had a few breakthroughs using magic, but the world just isn't ready for a magical fix."

She hadn't noticed that Tan had come closer. He reached out a hesitant hand and patted her head.

Right now, she really didn't want a platonic relationship. She'd never felt like this before. She'd always been accepting of her life. Mostly. Aisha had always looked at women who craved sex like they were crazy. Not that she was super experienced, but the few experiences she'd had made her battery powered friend more and more appealing.

The only orgasms she'd ever had were the ones she gave herself. Right now, though, her body wanted something, and he came in the form of a six-foot six man with arms the size of her thighs, and that was saying something. She was curvy, and the only gap her thighs had ever seen was when she was two. Not that her thighs weren't super helpful when you needed to choke a man out in self-defense class or holding a jar as you tried to pry the lid off of the pickles you desperately needed to stress eat at three am.

Stress and sex. Maybe that's why Deo looked so good. Sex was supposed to help with stress relief and crap was she stressed. Yeah, her panties were wet for a man she'd only seen a few times, and there was no chance he'd ever look at her twice.

But that was the thing. He did. He looked at her like he saw her, like he wanted her.

She needed a mental slap. Who cared? She was smart. Funny sometimes. And she was going to cure cancer, someday. She needed to move on. Restart tomorrow.

"Well, I am glad I came by. I thought I'd see if you wanted dinner?" Tan asked.

Aisha blinked. Right, Tan was here. The man that sparked a warmth of comfort, but nothing else. God. She needed to tell him. In the months since her father passed, it wasn't like they'd ever even kissed. Well, except the one night after the funeral. She'd been a little drunk, very depressed, and well he'd been there. But that was it. A kiss and it was like kissing her brother.

"Dinner? Uh. Sure. But then I'm going to need to come back to the lab."

He nodded. "Of course. Whatever you need."

Good guy. That's what Tan was. A good guy. He would let her spend days in her lab.

A knock at the door had them both looking as in walked her fantasy.

Aisha might have licked her lips as she watched him stride in in slow motion. His shirt was like a second skin. Every single muscle visible.

Oh, hell.

"Aisha? How are you?"

It took a minute to find her voice. Was she breathing heavily? Fantastic.

Blowing out a breath, she finally found the energy to fake a calm she sure as hell didn't feel.

"Hi, Deo. I'm good. You?"

He didn't look away, and she had to squeeze her thighs tight. Every time he was here his eyes swirled a strange gold and blue mix. There was something different, something not human.

Then again, wasn't that the case with most of those in Roswell? It's what drew her to this legendary city. Well, maybe legendary was the wrong word. That's okay.

"I'm fine. Thank you for asking. And your research?" he asked, his gaze flicking over the test tubes and slides.

She smiled. "It's slow. That poison you brought in isn't like anything I've seen. I've tried everything, and it's resistant to just about everything."

He nodded. "We think it has demonic properties. Not sure that helps at all."

Aisha's face fell. She was an idiot.

"Of course. I'm so stupid. Maybe if I'd tried harder in demonology courses."

She raced over to her cabinet that held random chemicals, some magical and some standard, opening up a cupboard just to let it slam as she moved onto another.

Someone cleared their throat. She rolled her eyes as she kept looking. Right, Tan and his social etiquette.

"Deo, meet Tan. Tan, Deo," she said over her shoulder.

Well, crap. She couldn't find what she wanted. A few years ago, she'd met a witch that taught her about demon makeup. Something like DNA, she supposed. Anyway, she had a small vial of a potion that could isolate the magic and nullify it. Where had she put it?

Turning back to Deo, she stopped dead as both men were locked in a staring competition.

Tan wasn't bad looking, but seriously, seeing them together he looked average. This was one of those moments where she really needed to think about her future. A loveless, although agreeable marriage without any passion assuming that kiss was any sign. Or did she hold out for something like she imagined, or rather, something she imagined with Deo.

Oh, right. Staring match.

"Have you two met or something?" she asked.

Neither turned to her.

"No. I can't say we have," Deo said.

"Yes. No. I'd remember someone like him. How do you know my Aisha?" Tan asked.

If it was possible, Deo might have just grown an extra inch and the veins in his neck popped.

"She is not yours, tiny human."

Aisha had the same thought, although she'd have worded it better.

"Tiny? Who are you calling tiny?"

Aisha's legs remembered how to work and she finally made her way over to the two men.

"You, human. I am calling you tiny. You would not satisfy her. You wouldn't satisfy one of those small creatures you call dogs."

Where the hell was this coming from? Deo said all of five sentences every time she saw him. She'd never have imagined this. Was he jealous?

Tan's caramel skin reddened, and Aisha flew into action.

"Whoa there, boys."

Stepping in between them, she pushed each away with the palm of her hand. With Deo, that was much easier said than done.

Absently, her fingers rubbed against Deo's chest. Okay, yeah. Maybe he was right, Tan wouldn't satisfy her when she had a taste for someone like him. But that wasn't fair. She just wasn't easy to please.

"Put the testosterone away. Do not have a pissing contest in my lab," she said.

Aisha looked up into Deo's face as his hand caressed hers. No fair. He was touching her. He wasn't supposed to touch her. Men didn't do that. Not even Tan.

"Hey, Aisha. He started it. What does he want?" Tan said, a whine in his voice that annoyed her.

Sighing, she turned to the one she'd promised her father she'd marry when her body screamed that this was all wrong. It screamed that she should be with Deo.

She swallowed a lump past her tight throat. Her body needed to shut up. He wouldn't want her. No, worse, she'd be breaking her promise to her dad. Still, keeping the annoyance out of her voice was impossible. She still wanted Deo, even if he was all wrong.

"I'm working with him, Tan."

Tan's nose curled up. "He sure seems a little, uh. Well, are you sure he's the thinking type? You know, with all those muscles?"

She snorted. "Really, Tan? That seems a little judge-y for a guy with a PhD in psychology. Aren't you supposed to be exactly the opposite of judgmental?"

His jaw muscles visibly tightened. "I'm not judging. I'm just saying, you don't see many like him."

Heat traveled up her arm as Deo's thumb traced a circle against her hand. What was she yelling at Tan about?

Oh, right.

Except Deo beat her to the punch.

"I am smart enough. I assure you," Deo said.

His voice sent chills down her spine. Why didn't he talk more? She could get used to this.

She pulled her hands away from both of them. If she didn't

stop touching Deo, she couldn't be held accountable for her actions.

She needed to clear her damn head.

She had a mission. She needed to finish her work. No distractions. No. No more love. Tan was safe, and if he ever died, it wouldn't break her. Sure, that was a sad reality and an even sadder truth. She'd miss his friendship, but it wouldn't break her, not like losing her dad.

Studying her hands, resenting the tingle still lingering on the one, she tried to snap out of it. Was that the worst reason to agree to a business-like marriage? Her father would be happy to know she wasn't alone. Too bad it all felt so wrong and every time she tried to think about kissing him again, a little throw up seemed to find its way into her throat.

God, she needed out of this situation.

"Tan, thanks. I'll meet you for dinner. Just text me where and as soon as I'm finished with Deo, I'll meet you. Okay?"

He looked at her and then looked at Deo. She felt like a child, a bit of nostalgia in the way Tan looked at her, the same way her father looked at her disapprovingly.

She missed him, but she wasn't sure she could agree to this marriage just for his sake. Yup, tonight, at dinner, she'd end it.

The memories of her father were close enough to a cold shower as she would need. At least it was safe for Tan to leave, even if she didn't voice that.

Tan nodded and finally headed to the door with a second glance before walking out.

Aisha left Deo standing in the middle of the lab as she headed back to her microscope, where one more failed trial lay. She had magic and science on her side, and yet she hadn't found a cure in time. Now what? She still wanted to save people from ever feeling the pain of watching someone suffer.

"Aisha?"

She looked up, realizing that her eyes were watering. She wouldn't admit they were tears.

"Do you cry because of that human?" Deo asked. He stepped forward, stepping around the table separating her from him.

Aisha didn't move. She couldn't help it, she wanted him near, but she didn't know why.

"No. It's not," she said, sniffling.

"Good. I don't like to harm humans, but I would make an exception."

His mouth watered to taste her. From the moment they'd seen her, Deo and his dragon knew she was theirs. They needed to wait, find the right time. Only, every moment he was near her seemed like it should be the right time. Except now.

Deo hated the way her eyes glistened. Tears, she was crying. He hated it. Why would she cry? Nothing had happened. He hadn't murdered the small male.

He squeezed his hands into fists at the memory. No, he hadn't. But damn, he'd wanted to.

His dragon snarled within him. Yes. They wanted to kill him, but Deo was too smart to let the rage consume him.

Now, all Deo felt was a fierce need to protect her.

He lifted a hand to her face and rested his palm against her cheek. She nuzzled against his warmth, allowing him to brush the tears away with his thumb.

"Why do you cry?"

A small idea of a smile tried to push its way onto her lips, but it lost and she frowned.

"My father. He's only been gone for six months and I'm still not over it."

Deo nodded.

"I feel like if I had had more time I could have saved him. And now..." she trailed off.

Deo felt the pain of regrets, of failure. This was all too familiar.

"I have lost someone. We all have. And, being the healer for my brothers and those we serve with, I feel that every death has been my fault. At some point you need to forgive yourself before you break."

Deo hadn't talked about his past often. His brothers knew, because sometimes they were in his head even if he didn't want them there. They were bound to each other in service, and sometimes you needed it. But, when you lost one, and it was your responsibility to stop the bleeding, the pain grew to be too much to forget.

He vowed he would never lose another of his brothers. Of course, that also meant he'd forgotten about himself. Until her.

Deo had fully expected coming to Earth would mean he would help each one of these idiots find their mates, and then fate had laughed in his face. How could he focus on them if his own dragon roared for its own mate? Her. This beautiful dark-haired beauty. His hands fucking ached with the need to grab her ass. He nearly moaned as he imagined kissing her full breasts.

Hell. At least she wasn't crying over that stupid little male. Although, that may have been easier to make her forget.

His dragon roared and Deo fought to keep control. Shit, is this what Eadric and Kal had gone through? No wonder they dealt with the shit their mates gave them. There was no choice.

Breathe.

What was something he could do? Keep her talking? Talk about what? It was better to understand the enemy as well, so perhaps he could use this moment to solve a few issues.

"What of that male? Does he need your help too?" Deo asked.

She blinked. The tears drying. He watched her. Was she going to explode again? Or was that it? Did females just stop like that? He'd have to ask Kal about this later.

"What? Oh, you mean Tan?" she asked.

Deo nodded. His jaw ached as he clenched it. "Why did he call you his?"

Deo stepped closer. She hadn't moved her face away from his touch, and his dragon was pushing the issue. Testing the boundaries.

He moved, but she did too. Aisha wouldn't meet his eyes, not yet. Why? Was she embarrassed? She shouldn't be. She stopped as her butt hit the counter behind them.

Good. He liked this.

"Look at me, Aisha," he said.

Her breasts rose and fell, her breathing growing more rapid the closer he seemed to get.

"I-" she paused as her gaze met his.

Deo was now close enough he could see every lash on her eyelids. He breathed in her scent, and the storm within him calmed. This was not what he'd planned. Why was he here? He'd only wanted to be near her. Breathe her in. He hadn't meant to corner her like prey, although truthfully, he enjoyed the hunt.

"Who is the male?" he asked, again.

"Tan is sort of my fiancé," she whispered.

Deo racked his brain for the human term. Fiancé. This word meant little to him. Fiancé?

Dipping his head, he lowered his face to the crook of her neck. She smelled heavenly. Sure, there was a chemical smell of her lab mixed with her own scent of a flowery mix. A feast to his senses.

Her heart picked up speed as he listened to her breathing. The air scented with the sweet aroma of her female mating scent. A hum of desire reverberated within his chest and she moaned.

"What is this fiancé?" he asked, as he gave in to the desire to taste her. Deo flicked his tongue along the soft skin of her neck.

Her voice came out breathy.

"I'm supposed to marry him."

Deo stopped and pulled away.

"Marry? As in you join your life with his?"

Her eyes opened. "What? Oh, yes. But-"

"No," he said.

She looked at him.

"What do you mean no?"

He growled. "I mean no. No, you do not join anything with him. No."

Her eyes grew wide. And perhaps this should have been a warning sign, but he didn't give one fuck right now.

"You. Are. Mine," he said.

Her lips made a flat line.

Yes, these were female warning signs. But she was his, damn it.

"Just who do you think you are? Just because you have muscles on top of muscles, does not mean you get to tell me anything. Mine? What does that even mean?" she asked.

Deo stood tall, but his brain went blank. She was questioning him? He was offering himself, and she was asking what he meant? He'd said mine. Wasn't that the word to end all words?

"Deo. Look. You seem nice and all."

He tensed as she ran her hands over his stomach. She must have noticed or realized what she was doing wasn't matching her words because she stopped.

"I'm not really in the market to get married. I'm really trying to get rid of that one. Tan just isn't right for me, but I'm not exactly looking for someone macho either. I mean, well."

She broke off and the scent of her arousal grew stronger. Maybe she said no, but her body called to him, saying something else entirely.

He leaned in again. This time he wouldn't stop. Marriage wasn't soul binding, it wasn't even physically binding from what he understood. People left all the time. He sniffed her again, and she squirmed.

She was still unspoken for. He could smell as much. There was no scent of a man or dragon on her. Unclaimed, and he didn't care if this wasn't an Earth custom, he wasn't going to be denied his soulmate.

She was his.

He bent and reached down, gripping the backs of her thighs and lifting her. He pressed Aisha against the unmistakable intent in his pants. Fucking pants. He liked the freedom of their battle kilts, but Earth required pants, or at least in this part of the world. Fine. He'd wear the things. But right now, he wanted to rip off her own clothing and bury himself deep within her.

She gave a surprised, "Oh" and he claimed her lips, cutting off anything else.

Slowly he released her lips, but not until her breathing was ragged and her body pressed into his in need.

Maybe he could get this mating thing done and move on to helping the rest of his brothers. This wasn't so bad.

"Wait. Stop," she panted.

He met her gaze. "Wait?"

Catching her breath, she finally spoke. "Wait. I might not want to marry him, but I don't want a one-night stand either."

He nuzzled her. "I am not asking for a one-night stand. I am offering you an eternity as my mate."

She nibbled her lower lip. Cute and super-hot was all he could think.

"So, you're a shifter then?"

Cocking his head, Deo once again found himself trying to remember what shifter meant. His brother, Kal, had told him about this Earth species. He preferred to be called a dragon warrior like he was, but if this is what made things easier. Fine.

"Yes. A dragon shifter. Much bigger than any of the Earth shifters you have."

Her head was nodding. "So shifters compete over size too, then? Wow. Men are all programmed the same."

Odd response, he thought.

"Compete over size? I wasn't. A dragon is simply larger than anything you have here. I am not aware of any land beasts that are larger. It's a fact that a dragon is much larger than most species on Earth. I can introduce you to him, but not in your lab."

She snorted a laugh.

"Are we still talking about this dragon?"

Scratching his head, Deo felt exactly the way his brothers had. Confused as all hell.

"Right. Yes. My dragon. He would like to meet his mate."

The laughter came out stronger until he had to back away. She was nearly doubling over, almost falling off the counter.

"Why is this funny?" he asked.

She sucked in some air and sat up. Her face flushed and her eyes sparkling. He liked that part. Deo liked how beautiful she was when she laughed, much better than the tears.

"I basically asked if you were talking about your dragon or your penis, and yeah. The look on your face, priceless. But, right. Dragons aren't real. So, what are you?"

He closed the gap.

"I am very real."

Deo let his dragon show through enough to get his point across, his eyes shifting between human and reptile.

She gasped. "So strange."

He smirked. "Is this a good strange?"

Lifting a hand to his face, she hesitated and then traced the soft skin along his temple down his cheek.

"I don't know," she said, studying him intently.

Deo nearly hummed in pleasure as she touched him.

A buzzing sound broke her concentration, and she peeked around. This was not going the way he'd hoped.

"Oh no. I promised Tan I'd meet him for dinner."

He quickly stepped forward, locking her between him and the counter again as he gripped her hips, keeping her in place.

"No." He shrank away as she glared.

"There's that word again. No. No. You don't own me, you do not tell me no," she practically scolded.

Deo growled. Something in him strangely turned on and attracted to the strength in this woman.

"But you are mine. Mating is merely a formality. You are mine. Fate has dictated it. You don't have dinner with another male."

She shifted, accidentally pushing up against his dick.

"Oh. I, uh," she said, fumbling over her words.

He smirked. "You what? Changed your mind?"

His nostrils flared; the scent of her need filled the air again. Yes. She wanted him. He just needed to try harder.

Leaning in, he kissed her. She squeaked, but didn't pull away.

An angry buzzing sounded again, and this time she pulled away and pushed him.

"Oh, for shit's sake."

He reached behind him, feeling along the island and knocking the damn comm to the floor. It stopped. Problem solved.

"Deo! That was my phone. You don't throw it. You push the little red dot. Damn it." Aisha wiggled free, accidentally brushing against him a few more times. He could do this the hard way as long as that happened more.

Aisha scowled as she wiggled free of him and reached down to pick up her communication device.

"You are so lucky I have a freaking industrial case on here. Gah. You shifters are all brawn and no brain."

She stopped and looked up at him.

"Sorry. That wasn't fair, was it? You were the one in here

talking about my research several days ago. I'm still sorry I didn't come up with an antidote."

They stood in silence, mostly because Deo wasn't entirely sure if he was supposed to speak or not. He could watch her. There was nothing like watching one's mate move.

"Is the girl okay?" she asked.

Girl? What girl? All he wanted was to sink his teeth into her and brand her as his.

"Deo? The girl? The one who was poisoned?" she asked again.

Oh. Right. Okay. He was supposed to speak then.

"Yes. Things did not go as expected, but in the end she is well."

His dick twitched as he watched her tongue dart out between her lips, licking her plump lower lip. He wanted more of her.

She looked down at her phone and punched something on the screen. "All right. Well, I need to get going."

He stepped forward.

"I will come as well," he said.

Abruptly she looked up.

"Wait. What?"

Deo stopped directly in front of her.

"I will come with you. Dinner sounds good. Do you plan to eat in a local establishment or are we to go to his dwelling?"

He bent down, wrapping an arm around her waist, his hand wandering down to her round bottom.

"I would enjoy seeing where you sleep, perhaps we go to your home?"

She shivered under his grasp and let out a shuttered breath. "It's at a restaurant. Nothing fancy."

He stood up straight.

"I will enjoy this. I have yet to eat with humans. Shall we?"

He smiled down at her as she opened her mouth just to close it again without saying anything else.

3

*A*isha flicked her gaze from one man to the other. Well, this was going well.

"So," she said.

Neither said anything.

"I thought that maybe I'd get dessert."

She waited for Tan to criticize her. What he lacked in passion, he tried to make up for in annoying knowledge. The latest of his obsessions was fad diets. If he tried to take her dessert one more time though, Deo would need to help bury the body.

Instead of Tan, though, she got Deo's two cents.

"I like this idea of dessert," he said.

Finally, Deo turned to her. And it was about damn time. Wasn't he here for her, supposedly?

"You would be delicious all over my mouth," he continued.

She choked on her water.

Once she caught her breath though, she wanted to scold him. Instead, the intensity of his gaze made her stop. She shivered as he licked his lips and her panties were suddenly wet.

A chair clattered, and she glanced over to Tan.

"Who do you think you are? She is my fiancé. You do not talk to her like that."

Aisha almost told him to shut up. Instead, she looked him dead in the eyes.

"Look, Tan. You're a nice guy. I value your friendship, but maybe we aren't really a good match? I meant to talk to you about that tonight. I mean, before he decided to-"

Decided to what? She didn't want to say crash the date, because secretly she actually didn't mind. Sort of. Aisha had been losing sleep over this conversation with Tan. Was it really the right thing to do? Would her father approve? Was she just being ridiculous?

Tan's mouth opened, but Deo's voice is what she heard.

"Perhaps we should find him a mate as well?"

Both Aisha and Tan turned to look at him.

"What?" she asked, trying to hide the surprise in her voice.

Deo shrugged. "You seem to worry that this male is alone. Perhaps we find him a mate as well."

Tan still hadn't spoken yet, and Aisha honestly wasn't sure how to react.

Was he for real? It wasn't a horrible plan, really. Or was it? Was she committed to letting her dad's last wish die with him? Just because she wanted to end things, didn't mean she actually ever really would. That was the bigger issue. If she didn't ever actually follow through on ending the agreement, she'd just let Tan talk her back into whatever because she was so emotionally tired.

Glancing at Deo, she figured maybe if he tried and succeeded then it wouldn't be on her.

"You mean a girlfriend? Humans don't mate, Deo," she said.

The longer she thought about it, the more she liked this plan. Why hadn't she thought about that, hire someone to find Tan his soulmate or well, anyone really? It would get rid of the guilt of not wanting him. Also, maybe he'd find someone who would make him happy.

A heaviness sat in her chest. The agreement had been that she wouldn't be alone. But Deo had said he was offering himself. That counted, right? And it wasn't like Deo seemed to mind she was emotionally unavailable.

Emotionally unavailable yes, but dang it if her body wasn't vibrating with energy every time Deo was around. That screamed she most definitely wouldn't be alone if he had any say in it.

"I already had her father find me someone, she's right there. Why would you do any better?" Tan said, pointing at Aisha.

Aisha squirmed under Deo's attention.

"I do not claim to be better at anything, but she is wrong for you. I believe that if one is open, listens to his soul, his mate will find him. Just as Aisha has," Deo said, never turning his attention away from her.

There were literally so many things wrong with this moment she didn't know where to start. Looking between the two, she started with Deo.

Her mind was at odds with her heart, and the fact was her libido didn't care about either of them.

Tan stomped his foot like a toddler. That didn't help his case. His brotherly appeal went up while husbandly appeal pretty much just fell off a cliff headfirst and started on fire.

"Tan, I. Uh. Why don't I walk you home and then I'll talk with Deo later? Okay?"

Deo scowled, but she ignored it. Or she tried to. Was he growling?

"I will walk this male home, you will not be alone with him," scolded Deo.

Pinching the bridge of her nose, she tried to envision this going worse. Did she tell him how weird that sounded? Did she argue about him taking away her freedom to walk with someone she'd walked with before?

He reached across the table, his hand resting on her free one.

Maybe she should start by telling him to remove his hand before she came in public? No, probably not that one.

"Deo…" she hung her head. "Never mind. Let's go."

Aisha got up and walked to the doors and if the men followed, then whatever. She didn't care. Aisha didn't need the guilt of Tan, and she didn't need the distraction of Deo.

The heat of the late day sun hit her face as she stepped out onto the sidewalk. Aisha could practically feel Deo's gaze burning a hole in her back. She turned around to wait for them and stepped into the wall of Deo. Breathing in, she instantly wanted to bury her face in his shirt more. Deo had followed because of course he had, and he hadn't left much space between them either.

"Have you ever heard the phrase personal space?"

A stoic stare looked down at her. Right. Dragon shifter or something.

Maybe they weren't around people much. With looks like his, he probably had to fight off mobs of women. So, maybe he just didn't care.

A small piece of her was beginning to believe his crazy story. He talked strangely; he said human instead of person a lot, and he wasn't like any shifter she'd ever met before.

She started to walk down the street, trying to decide how she really felt about Deo. Maybe she was blinded by his charm. Good-looking only got you so far if you were really bat shit crazy. Only, she wasn't sure he was.

There was something more. Aisha thought back to a few days ago, remembering what he'd been like. Different from this possessive man in front of her.

The way he'd run into her office, nearly begging to know what kind of chemistry she specialized in. He'd looked half crazed with desperation, or well as much as his stone exterior ever looked crazed. He didn't have many facial expressions, or maybe there just wasn't much that got to him. His eyes, though. His eyes said everything, and all she had to know was what to look for.

This had all started when he'd thrust an odd little chip at her. Aisha had been honest that she didn't understand technology, but he hadn't needed her for that. No. He wanted to know about the residue, a poison apparently.

The truth was, Aisha would have helped him out of curiosity, but the way he'd looked at her, like he'd just found something he hadn't expected, stopped her in her tracks.

Or maybe it had been the way her heart had fluttered, and something within her screamed that he was who she needed. Yeah. It was that damn feeling that had gotten her derailed from her own research.

She needed to help him. It wasn't a question; it was a soul deep desire and when she failed, a part of her nearly died. Only the big, tough, stone-faced man hadn't been angry. He'd been the opposite. Thankful even, and then he'd continued to stop by.

"What if I don't want him knowing where I live, Aisha?"

Oh, right. She wasn't alone. In fact, she had two men who both seemed to want her attention. When had that ever happened? Never. She'd either been so single that even her couch had put half of itself up for rent, or she'd settled for someone that she'd choose a dry piece of toast over. What was this world coming to?

"Seriously, Tan? He knows where I work. If he wanted to stalk anyone, it would be me. Not you. I'm pretty sure you aren't his type."

Wow. She rubbed her temple with her fingers. That might have been a little snippy, but this is what you got when she was confused, horny, and maybe a little irritated.

They continued to walk. Tan didn't deserve to think she'd

cheated, or that she had already replaced him. That's what this was starting to feel like, though. She should have pushed Deo to stay away, only she wasn't sure that even putting up a fight would have stopped him.

She slowed as they got closer to the house.

"Deo, can you give us a second? I need to talk to Tan. Alone."

She blew out a breath, hoping it helped her nerves. If her dad had known that she'd find someone else, he never would have set her up in an arranged marriage. Most likely.

Or maybe he would have. He had married for love and it hadn't worked out for him. Aisha didn't think much of her mom. She'd left long before Aisha had even come into her magic. Her dad never seemed to get over it, but then again, he said the reason she'd left was him. Insecurity that she'd leave him, a human, for someone better.

Gah. She needed out of her head.

Glancing at the house, she focused on what would happen if she broke things off with Tan? It was her house, but he rented her basement apartment, and she enjoyed that. Who wouldn't want a friend close by?

She pursed her lips as Deo got closer. How did she even know that without looking? Who knows? But her body was hypersensitive to him, that was clear.

"Deo, that is the opposite of giving me space," she said.

He grunted. "I have excellent hearing. I don't see any reason to walk away."

Dragging in a breath of air through her nose, Aisha realized sarcasm was lost on the big guy. This was why she wasn't married yet, or well that's what dad had said. She was too much for any man. Only he'd found Tan and as much as her dad had loved her, he'd also made her feel like this was the best she could do.

Medium height, handsome, and not her type. Ha. Apparently, her type was out-of-her-league hot with muscles for days. Yeah.

She had lofty standards for someone who didn't feel like she fit anywhere.

Looking at Deo, she shook her head again. "Okay. Fine. I don't care if you hear, but could you just pretend? Maybe go sniff that tree or something."

She watched the wheels turn and if he said one more thing; she was going to lose it. Aisha couldn't put off Tan anymore, and come to think of it, she wasn't sure she could deal with "possessive" dragon guy either.

"Fine. I will walk over there. I don't sniff trees, but also, I will be looking for a mate for this male. There are many females here."

"Okay. Fine, whatever."

Deo finally walked away, and Aisha felt like she could breathe again. When he was around, it seemed like the world revolved around him and all the air in the world was anchored to him.

But as he walked away, her mind cleared enough to focus on Tan.

"Look, Tan. I'm sorry about this. He's a really nice guy. I've heard about shifters, and apparently, they get possessive. I don't really know why, well, I mean, I can guess," she stopped.

Tan looked around her, which wasn't like him. He was nice, and he always felt like eye contact was the best way to communicate. Even if sometimes she had to look at his nose because the staring contest was too much.

"Tan? Look at me, I'm trying to figure out how to make-"

"Uh, Aisha?"

Rolling her eyes, she answered. "Yes, Tan?"

"I think he's going into that house?"

"What?" She spun on her heel and her jaw dropped as she watched Deo talking to one of her slutty neighbors. She'd never said more than one word to this single woman because her tiny bikini-clad body in the front yard made Aisha want to punch her. Yeah. It was judge-y, but seriously. Why couldn't she sunbathe in the backyard? Maybe she was nice? Honestly, Aisha never had time to figure it out. Based on that, she'd just let some strange man in her house, yeah. No. She didn't think she was the brightest.

"You're seeing this? That your admirer knocked on that door and now he's going in."

Yeah. She was seeing it and her face heated. He was not going into that house. Aisha glared as she power-walked across the street, reaching the door as it clicked closed.

Knocking on the door with fervor, she might have put a little more gusto into the knock than expected.

The bimbo answered. "Hi?"

Aisha smiled sugary sweet. "I think my friend is lost and just came in here. I want him back."

Deo peeked around the door.

"Aisha, here is a female."

She turned her eyes up, trying really hard to not slap something.

"Deo, please come here."

He didn't hesitate and came, turning to the girl. "I had hoped to see if perhaps you were compatible for a male. I was mistaken though, your scent is all wrong."

The woman's eyes grew wide. "Your scent is off," she quipped back.

Deo shrugged. "You are not my soulmate. This matters very little to me."

Aisha let her temper get the best of her as she walked forward, pointer finger at the ready. "He smells amazing. And who cares what you think, you let some strange man into your house. Who does that?"

No one said anything mean about her Deo. Aisha swallowed. Oh, no. She'd jumped from wanting to have sex with him, to finally finding courage to break off her fake engagement with Tan, to apparently accepting his claim that she was his.

No. No. No. That wasn't how this went. But then again, as she watched the woman eyeing Deo, Aisha could feel a jealous rage trying to peek out behind her normally cool exterior.

"Whatever. A guy like this knocks on your door, and maybe you're willing to see where it goes? Besides, I watched through my window and saw him talking to you in the street. I figured he couldn't be all bad if he was talking to you. But, whatever. I don't even know what that means, that my scent is wrong. If he's one of those Area 51 nuts or something, then yeah. You can have him back. I don't care how sexy you are, I'm good."

The door slammed, and Aisha grabbed his arm.

"What are you doing? How did you even get her to let you in?"

They were halfway across the street before she realized his hand was in hers as she dragged him behind. He could have stopped her at any point, and yet he let her.

They were almost on the curb in front of her house when he finally stopped and walked away again.

Good Lord, What now?

"Deo, stop."

He didn't. She watched him as he strolled on a mission.

"She is unmated, Aisha. I will be back," he threw the words over his shoulder.

She threw her hands up and shook her head.

"He's determined, isn't he?"

She narrowed her eyes as he approached a woman on the sidewalk.

"Shut up, Tan. This is your fault."

Did she just sit on the curb and let this happen? What the hell? He apparently took the mission to get Tan a girlfriend seriously. This was going to be a really long night chasing him and trying to keep him out of jail.

"He's apparently really into you if he's trying to get someone for me this fast. Also, it's kind of strange. How does he know she's unmated?"

This time she squeezed her hands tight and struggled to not break her teeth as she mashed them together.

"I have no idea, Tan. He says he's a dragon shifter or something."

Tan put his hand on her shoulder. "If he's a shifter, you probably should just give up now. As a human I don't get it, but I think we all know the rumors. The fated mates thing isn't something you ditch. My cousin mated a tiger shifter and yeah. She's pretty happy."

"Well, Mr. Expert. What do you think you're going to say to this girl following him? How does he do that, anyway?" She mumbled that last part. How the hell was she supposed to compete if he could literally talk to any female and have them follow. Who was he?

"Tiny male. Remove your hand from my mate."

Tan's hand slid off her shoulder, and she just glared. Deo had such a god complex, and frankly she was just pissed he seemed to get what he wanted. "Don't call him that, Deo. He doesn't call you 'huge male'."

Deo ignored her. "Male, meet this female. Her name is Tess, and she is not mated."

The girl giggled.

"Deo, you can't just walk up to any woman and assume they will get along."

Tan waved to the girl, while Aisha grabbed Deo's hand and tugged. "Deo, a word, please."

He looked at the girl, and Aisha couldn't help the spike of jealousy.

"Excuse him. We'll be right back."

The girl smiled as Aisha stomped away, dragging Deo a few houses down.

"What are you doing?"

She wanted to be mad, but when he smiled her entire body thrummed with energy and need.

"She would make a good mate. She smells pure and matches his scent patterns. Plus, she has a wonderful butt just like yours."

There was literally nothing she could say to that. Because, well. She would either be pissed he looked at the girl's ass or flattered that he liked hers.

Damn it, if she wasn't tied in one big knot.

4

*D*eo cautiously approached his future mate as her eyes narrowed to slits. She opened her beautiful pink mouth and then closed it several times. Perhaps she was mad. Sniffing the air, the spicy scent of her anger filled the air and mixed with the delicious scent of her need. How could she be angry and aroused all at once? Perhaps he didn't care. His dragon roared with a need to claim their mate.

Deo fought the shift against the beast. If he didn't, the dragon would probably just take her and hide her away until she gave into their human side. That worked for Eadric though, but not without a lot of issues first. No. He would do this the civilized way.

He could imagine what she might look like as he buried himself deep within her. Perhaps he wasn't as civilized as he was pretending. Because damn it, he prayed to the goddess she'd be his soon.

Mentally he went down the checklist of things that should be simplifying the process. He had already found a woman that held similar physical qualities as his Aisha, and therefore that male should be fine. Even if he wasn't, Deo didn't really fucking care right now.

Damn. Her face was still squinched, her nose making an adorable little wrinkle on her brow that he wanted to kiss away. Why the hell was she mad? God, he should have listened to his brothers. Earth women made no sense.

"Deo, you can't just pick a woman because she's chubby. You also can't go around sniffing women, that's rude. Or, well, it sounds rude."

His brow furrowed. "What does chubby mean? If it is regarding your ass, then why can't I pick a woman with equally delightful assets?"

Her upper lip curled.

"Okay. What are you? Where the heck are you from? No. Chubby doesn't mean delightful, or well …" Aisha stood a little taller and her face smoothed out.

This was better, but he still enjoyed the fire in her eyes. He couldn't control himself. He wanted to listen to her words, but right now her temper was turning him on. One quick move and she was against him, his mouth claiming her lips, swallowing whatever else she was about to say. She needed to be quiet so he could taste her.

She mumbled something and maybe punched him once before she relaxed into his embrace and started kissing him back.

Deo fought back the urge to take her. His dragon wanted control. He was well aware that forcing a mate did not end well on this planet or any other.

Slowly, he pulled his lips away. "You were saying?"

She blinked at him several times. "You can't just go grab a woman-"

He smiled. "Is this you complaining then?"

Her beautiful full mouth pouted for a moment. "You're an

asshole. God, no wonder my dad decided I needed help with finding someone. Granted-"

They both turned to look back at Tan. He and the female were talking. Deo sniffed the air.

"They find each other mutually acceptable. Shall we go now?"

He looked down at her. She wasn't blinking. "Did you have a heart-attack mate?"

Her head whipped around. "What? No. Don't call me that either. But how do you know that they are attracted to each other?"

He put a finger to the side of his nose. "Scent. Their arousal is very obvious. You, however, still have a spicy scent around you, the scent of anger. Why are you angry? Isn't this what you wanted?"

Her words came out slow. "Yes. But. He was supposed to marry me. Am I that easy to forget?"

Deo wrapped his arms around her, pulling her into him.

"He will not marry you, because you are mine."

She didn't even look at him.

Odd. He thought that would have more allure.

"Yeah. Okay. Whatever. But still," she mumbled.

Thoughts ran through his head. How would he win her? Also, she didn't exactly seem excited about the prospect of being his mate. Again, he should have listened to his brothers better.

"Would you like to see my dragon?"

That got her attention. "What?" she squeaked, finally looking at him instead of that other male.

"My dragon? Would you like to meet him?"

Her mouth moved, but she said nothing for a second.

"Uh. Isn't that like a second date kind of thing?" she said.

Date? What was a date? He reached out to his brothers.

It's a human custom. Males take females out for food and entertainment, Eadric thought back.

Ah.

"No. It could be an any date kind of thing," he said, mimicking her words.

He watched as her brow lifted.

"I'm trying to be open-minded. But I don't care how hot you are, I don't want to see your 'dragon'."

Deo was certain they had a language barrier. This might have been similar to Kal's misunderstanding, and damn it if he didn't want to be turned into a chicken. He started to pull away, but her hands shot out.

"I didn't say you had to back away. I mean, it's cold."

Taking a deep breath, Deo tried to understand what was going on.

"I will not then. But I don't know that you understand when I say 'dragon'. I'm a dragon shifter. Like your wolves I've heard of. There are lots of wolf shifters in this area."

The thrum of her heart reached his ears as her scent lost some of the spicy scent of anger.

"Oh," was all she said, finally turning to look at him. Maybe she was finally forgetting the other male.

Deo allowed his dragon to surface just enough. His eyes shifted between his human form and his beast's. His eyesight grew clearer. The beat of her heart grew louder, and the heat of her body took on a reddish hue. His skin took on the blue hue of his dragon and scales appeared over skin.

"Oh, is that-" she paused.

"Yes, that's my dragon."

He pulled in her scent once again. His dragon didn't enjoy being cooped up, away from his mate, but Deo knew that this was not the right time. He was smarter than Kal and Eadric, or he'd like to think he was. He was the more mindful one, the one who understood people and those around them. His strength was emotion. Except for hers. He sucked when it came to his own mate.

"So, that's real. Dragons. And that girl I helped? The one you brought to the lab?"

He shook his head. "She is not a dragon, although she is the mate of Eadric. We aren't sure exactly what she is outside of human."

A slow nod was all he got at first.

"The magic side of me could tell some of her genetic makeup is human, some of it is demon. I've seen it before in a lab. Before I abandoned working for a magical university, they were big on trying to understand demon chemical makeup. It's a big thing in the magical communities. Learn how to control a whole other realm of power," she said.

He couldn't hide a rumble of disgust. "No one should control demons. No one should control anyone, but demons especially. Even the ones that control the lesser, more unpredictable breeds struggle."

Aisha nodded. "Yeah. I agree. It's why I left. Well, that and my dad."

Deo was all ears. He wanted to know about her. Know what made her who she was.

"What about your father?"

Her eyes dimmed as she spoke. "He got sick. Cancer. It's not something a shifter would understand, but he was human. My mother abandoned us when I was little, and he was all I had."

Deo had heard of diseases here on Earth. He'd found the frailty of the human race fascinating and also a bit worrisome when looking for mates. He was worried that all the information they'd known was wrong. What if these humans couldn't withstand their dragon's magic? What if their mate was sick and their magic couldn't overcome the illness? What if their mates didn't exist at all?

Thousands of years of traditions and every generation of Amit dragon warrior had new battles to face. Apparently he and his brothers faced sassy women from Earth.

"I understand the sadness in your eyes all too well. I'm sorry."

She sniffled, and her words were choked. "My father lost his battle, and I wish I could have stopped it."

Deo's chest ached for her, not just because she was his mate, but also because he understood what it was to lose someone and not have been able to do a thing about it.

"I am sorry, my Aisha. I'm sure he still looks over from the afterworld. The goddess has a plan for all of us."

Deo reached for a tear trailing down her cheek, catching it with his finger. Goddess, what could he do?

Bending down, he kissed the spot where the tear had been. Deo didn't want to see her hurting, but sometimes things were beyond even what he could fix. Gently, he cradled her chin and captured her eyes with his own soft stare.

"I would kiss away your sadness, if you'd let me."

She swallowed. "I... I don't want to feel this pain anymore. I don't want anyone to ever feel this pain again. I want to save lives. This is why I took my fellowship here."

She bit her lower lip and sniffled again. "And now even that might go away. I wanted to combine magic and science to find something. But my grant request was denied, and even my colleagues have abandoned me. At least-"

She stopped and looked back at the human male. "Even Tan is easily swayed away from me."

Deo titled his head, watching the human male and the woman. He then looked back at Aisha.

"I have not abandoned you. I believe in your work. I knew it from the moment I laid eyes on you. You would change my world, and yes, I believe you will change this one."

Aisha turned her head back to him, looking up, and blinking several more tears away.

"I don't understand you half the time, but when I am here," she stopped, and placed her hand to his chest. "I feel the truth in your words. But how do I know that what you say isn't just what

I want to hear? Have you ever heard of criminals being experts at what they do? Knowing how to prey on people or finding jobs in the field to access what they need? How do I trust you?"

Deo thought about it. He'd never been asked how one was to know trust. You just did. A dragon warrior was bound by his word and by his honor. If one were to lie, it could jeopardize the mission. Even with honor, sometimes the fight didn't end well, but at the very least they would die a hero.

"I am bound by my word. Honor is all I have to offer, for now."

She shivered in his embrace.

"What does that mean? For now?" she asked.

Visions of her naked, splayed out for his taking, flashed in his mind. "Once I claim you, once you are mine, nothing would be a secret. My heart and my soul would be yours." He covered her hand with his own. "My mind would be open for you to explore. I have nothing to hide."

She didn't look away from him. "What," she cut herself off and licked her lips before continuing.

"What exactly does claiming involve? Like, what do you have to do?"

Wrapping an arm around her, Deo pulled her against him. It was a good sign she was open to talking to him. Maybe she felt what he did? Or perhaps she was at least starting to.

"I would start by kissing you. Like this," he said, gently touching his lips to hers.

"Yes," she said, her eyes closing as he moved down her chin.

"Then I would touch you here," he said, as he moved his hand between her legs.

Her eyes flew open, and he smirked at her surprise.

"I would pleasure you until you screamed my name." His words were barely a whisper.

Deo kissed her jawline down to the soft skin of her neck as she tilted her head, inviting him for more. Once he got to her collarbone, he shifted his position. Moving his hand to the neck of her shirt and pulling it aside.

Licking the space between her neck and her shoulder, he spoke. "Here is where you would bear my mark."

He liked the way her breathing hitched and her chest pressed against him as she inhaled.

"But, for now. I've asked you to trust me and you do not. So, let me show you trust. Should we go on a date? Perhaps back to your lab and look at specimens? I would do anything to see you smile."

He would do anything to keep her, and if that meant earning her trust, he would do what he had to.

5

*A*isha couldn't look away. She didn't want to look away. His eyes were endless, like they held the answer to everything in her world. What would happen if she stopped thinking, just this once? Let him have her.

If anything, her body might enjoy the release. But what if she believed him? Dragon shifter, it sounded real. Paranormal beings were everywhere, hiding in plain sight. Who was to say that dragons hadn't mastered this ability?

Who was she to deny the heat coursing through her body? Her own magic had come to life the day he'd walked into her lab. Suddenly she had made headway on some things, even if it had come too late to secure that damn grant. She wanted to believe that it was because of Deo.

She wanted to forget more than anything. Would a few hours of being his, whatever that meant, let her forget? God, what would it be like to let him do as he so boldly implied?

The trail of heat he left between her legs had woken up more than just a few nerve endings. A burn of desire settled between her legs and she wasn't sure she could stop the need no matter how hard she tried.

If he let her go, she'd collapse. Her legs were weak, a wobble setting in with her nerves. She'd known Tan for months longer and yet, she'd never felt like she knew him. Deo though, she saw everything in his eyes, and she couldn't understand why.

"Is it always like this?" she asked.

A hand against her back held her tighter.

"Is what always like this?"

She had to think. What the hell had she meant? Lust? No, she'd had that a few times in her life. What had he called it, mating? Claiming? What did those mean? She didn't actually know any shifters, not really.

"This? Love?" Her heart hammered away, and she was positive he could feel it. She said the word, love. Is that what she meant? Was that what this was?

God, his eyes. They were such an odd shade of an orange and blue that swirled. No, he wasn't human.

"This is much deeper than what you define as love. What I offer is my soul. Your soul recognizes its true mate and no, it is different for each of us. One thing is always true, though. We know our mate the moment we see her."

The world swam a bit. Oh crap, she'd been holding her breath.

"I, what about that date?" she asked.

Oh, gees. Had she just asked him out? He'd offered her sex, which she was positive would be mind-blowing if the bulge pressing against her stomach was any indication, but no. She'd just basically cock blocked herself.

"Aisha? You're okay?" Tan asked.

Nope, Tan had just cock blocked her. Where the hell had he just come from?

"I. Yeah. All is fine."

The sound of footsteps against the pavement had her pushing away from Deo.

She was still engaged. Right? Or had she just agreed she was fated to be Deo's?

Damn it. What did any of this mean? If her soul belonged elsewhere could she really and truly actually have gone through with marrying someone else? Maybe this was why she could never see him, or anyone else as more than just a friend.

Her soul was a bitch.

Damn it, Dad! She wanted to curse her father next for being human. If he'd been something paranormal. Anything other than human. He'd still be here, and she wouldn't have agreed to marry a stranger. Okay. He wasn't a total stranger. They'd met when they were two, before her father had moved them away.

That wasn't what love was supposed to be. This was the modern world, and she wasn't held to any standards being a half witch, half human. She was supposed to be free of all social expectations, not fitting into either world. Except, her father still believed in traditions. He still believed his daughter needed to be cared for. Arranged marriages still existed for her father.

"Aisha?"

Shit, Tan was still here. She looked at him. "Yes? Where's your new friend?"

His hands were in his pockets. "Home? But I wondered if we should go inside?"

Her eyes grew wide at the murder written all over Deo's face.

Her mouth dropped as she watched in an almost slow-motion moment as Tan turned and started to run. Deo a blur in her eyesight as he chased him down.

"Shit. Stop. Deo, stop."

Damn. She'd never seen a man move so fast, and she meant Tan. Deo was a fucking freight train. Tan had motivation.

Aisha took off after them, trying to catch them at least until her legs burned and her damn boobs hurt from bouncing.

Wrong fucking bra today, that was for sure. Had she known she would be running, she'd have worn some kind of sports bra, not that they ever worked. That's why she never exercised, that and being too busy at the lab. Hell, who was she kidding. She didn't exercise because she wasn't built for it.

"Deo," was the only word she got out as she took one, two, three more steps and officially stopped. Oh, Lord. She was having a heart attack. This had to be a heart attack.

No. No, that was what it felt like when you pushed a body that called climbing two flights of stairs cardio. Her hand rested on her chest as she tried to will her heart to slow the hell down.

"Deo." She tried again.

He finally stopped a few blocks away, the black dot in the night the only thing she could make out. Tan was definitely the smaller dot.

"Deo, stop. He lives in my basement."

Oh God. The world was spinning. She put a hand out as she sunk to the ground. Oh, Lord. She couldn't catch her breath. Yeah. No. She needed to get back to running. Strike that. She needed to start. Right after she took a little nap. Here. In the middle of the street.

"Are you all right?"

Aisha looked up from her street view at the Deo tower.

"Weren't you just like a mile away?"

He looked back down the street. "Perhaps? Does it matter?"

She shook her head. "Yeah. No. Whatever. You're a dragon."

Holding out a hand, he offered her help to get up. Lifting her lead arm, or well it seemed to be lead at the moment, she struggled to grip his hand.

"Yeah. No. I need a second. I don't do this running thing. Also, stop chasing off people. Tan lives in my basement apartment. I rent it out for extra income and well, when Dad brought him here, he needed a place to stay."

Deo eyed her. "Your basement?"

She leaned against her hands.

"Yes, you crazy ass dragon man. The part of my house built

underground. It could be storage, but mine is a small apartment. Lord. I think I'm dying."

Deo kneeled next to her and put two fingers up to her neck.

What was he doing now?

"No. Your pulse seems normal. I would say you are fine."

Okay. She didn't actually mean she was dying.

"Right. Okay. Thanks. Well, once my legs stop shaking you can walk me home."

Deo nodded. "Yes. Also, should I retrieve that male? So you can tell him you don't need him?"

She squinted in the night distance. "Uh, yeah. No. I think he's making good time. He's probably circling back anyway, since you know. Home's over there."

Aisha hated to admit the next feeling. Pride? No. Giddy excitement? Maybe. Mr. Sexy-dragon *had* just chased someone over her. Sure, maybe it had been strange. But still.

It felt kind of good.

Deo reached for her. "If you'll let me, I will carry you home?"

"Oh. Okay." She wrapped her arms around his neck, and he lifted her. This was new, and she liked it.

She really liked that she didn't need to try to make her legs function again for a few minutes.

6

Deo stood on her porch, listening to her lock the door. He would not leave until she was safe. Or at least until he knew that Tan would not be coming back.

He expected to hear her feet as she walked away, doing whatever it was a woman might do. But instead, a soft rustle against the door caught his attention.

He sniffed the air. She was still there. Still close. He put his hand up against the wood, as if he could feel her through the surface. The dragon in his head snarled. She was so close. They could take her. She wasn't leaving. She was close. She was staying. They could claim her.

Deo fought back the need for her. His muscles burned with restraint against his dragon, who was pissed they were waiting. His dick throbbed. Denying what he was meant to do sucked. She was his.

His hand shifted from dragon claw back to human as he argued with his soul. He would not push her. Again, Kal had proved that point. Eadric, however, he'd taken things slower. Much slower and it had paid off. Deo would learn from them.

Maybe. His dragon's claws dragged against the wood as he pulled them away.

The door swung open and inside was Aisha, breath-taking, flushed. Deo felt his own breath catch. Goddess, he wanted her.

He wasn't strong enough to resist. Before he knew what he was doing, he grabbed her up and kissed her like his very life depended on it. And perhaps it did. She healed the ache within him. The ache of loss and failure and the fear of losing himself to the dragon.

She wrapped her legs around his waist as he walked inside the doorway, slamming the door closed behind them with a kick.

She tasted like heaven. Deo couldn't stop his hands from wandering, gripping her ass as he pressed her into the wall. She moaned against his mouth as he pressed his aching dick against her. He would not hide his intentions. He wanted her, needed her. God, he needed her.

The scent of her arousal pushed him forward. She wanted him.

Running his hand over her back, up her side, he rubbed his palm over her breast, feeling the taut peak under the fabric of her shirt. He gently pinched the nub and enjoyed the moan it elicited.

He growled at the fabric. There were entirely too many layers between him and his mate.

Clenching his teeth, he fought the need to mark her. It wasn't time, not yet. But he could take the edge off a bit. A moan rose in his chest as her hand slipped down his waistband.

Fuck.

He broke the kiss, dragging in a breath of air.

Goddess, her touch.

She pulled her hand out of his pants and frantically started yanking at the snap.

He wanted to tell her to stop. He needed to work on the trust he'd promised her but fuck it.

Claiming her lips once again, he lowered her feet to the ground, giving him better access to her own pants. They needed to go and now. His dick sprang free as she lowered his zipper, and he nearly lost it as she grazed her hand over the head.

No. He would pleasure her over and over. And only then would he allow himself to come.

She kicked off her shoes as he released the button of her pants and yanked at the zipper. She wiggled out of the fabric and frantically went back to working on him.

Her soft palm grazing the soft sensitive skin of his hard on. He breathed through the pleasure and desire before he lost control and grabbed at her hips, lifting her again. He did not want to wait.

Running his hand between them, slicking his fingers in her juices as he slid a finger down her slit, spreading her, Deo explored Aisha. He found her sensitive nub and rubbed it between his thumb and finger. Her hips bucked against him. Sliding his fingers lower, he found her entrance and slipped a finger in, eliciting a whimper from her soft swollen lips.

As he stroked her, Deo slid in a second finger. She began to pant under his touch, and her muscles quivered around his fingers. He pulled his fingers out and rubbed her slick heat against his own hard on.

"Yes," she moaned.

Deo needed no other invitation to quench his own throbbing need.

With one quick thrust, he pushed in, her tight muscles stretching around him. He bit back his own groan of pleasure. Her legs tightened around his waist in answer to the new pace he set, all need and desire. Instinct.

He kissed her again, swallowing her cries as he thrust in over and over. She felt so good. He wanted her need to mirror his own; he wanted her desperate for him.

His hands gripped her ass and lifted her, pulling her down against him, increasing the pressure. He would make her want him over and over again.

After a few minutes, he couldn't stop himself as she let out a cry as the muscles between her legs, her core, pulsed around his shaft. He pushed into her once more, and only then did he allow himself to spill into her. Perhaps his dragon wouldn't be happy they didn't fully claim her, but he wouldn't mark her for now. She would bear his scent. And that would have to be enough for tonight.

Resting his forehead against hers, their breathing came rapidly for a few more moments.

He didn't want to leave her; he didn't want to stop.

"Want to come upstairs?" she asked between pants of air.

A smile he couldn't stop crossed his lips.

"What is upstairs?" he asked.

Aisha looked away. "Uh. My bed?"

Yes, Deo liked this idea very much.

"If you put me down, I can show you?" she asked.

He pulled out and lowered her to the ground; her legs shaky as he held her for another moment.

"I have never done this before," she said, finally looking up at him.

Deo stood a bit taller. Her words pleased him.

"I mean, I've done it. But I've never done this. I- "she stopped for a minute and ran her hand through her hair.

"Is sex always this good with you?" There was a giggle in her voice as she looked around and grabbed up her pants.

Deo stepped away and tucked himself back into his own pants.

"Nothing is ever as good as it is with your fated mate. With you, it will always be better. Our bodies were made for each other."

Watching her, she nibbled her lower lip as she seemed to contemplate something.

"Well. I don't actually know that fate is real, but I do know that I've never felt like that before. I've never had an orgasm during, you know. And just wow."

Watching her talk, Deo's mouth already watered for another taste of her. He stepped forward and kissed her. As he pulled away, he whispered in her ear. "Well, show me your bed and I can make up for lost time."

An encouraging hitch in her breathing had his pants growing tight again.

She turned away, pulling him along by his hand.

"I can't believe I'm doing this," she whispered.

Deo pulled her back, stopping her.

"You do not have to do anything. I will do all the work."

She gave a little hiccup laugh.

"That's not what I meant."

Deo closed the gap. He wanted to erase the unease. Mates were meant for each other. Time had no meaning. It didn't matter if you'd met an hour or a year ago; you were meant to be, and fighting it did nothing but make the hunger for the other worse. The goddess had known what she was doing, except that she had made life rather difficult for her chosen.

"You are not doing anything that isn't meant to be. Denying me is like denying your soul's deepest desires."

He placed his hand over her heart.

"The goddess designed us to love, to connect ourselves with the one that grounds us and keeps us connected to our humanity. Without you, I would cease to exist as you see me now. The magic too much for my soul to control alone. You, Aisha, are my chosen one."

The sound of their breathing filled the silence as she studied him. He opened his soul to her. He'd allow her more if she found the courage to love him.

His eyes shifted from human to dragon as he watched her, his soul searching, trying to allow her the proof she needed to trust.

Aisha raised her hand, resting her palm against his cheek. He nuzzled into the warmth of her touch.

"For tonight, let your soul do the feeling." He touched her temple gently. "This has a tendency to ruin the things our hearts know."

Raising on her tip-toes, she reached for him. He met the silent call of her lips with his own. This time the kiss was soft, desperate for the touch rather than the release.

He lifted her again and walked up the stairs without breaking their connection.

As they reached the landing, she pulled away. "That room, there," she said and pointed.

He licked her earlobe and grabbed her ass as he moved toward her room.

The interior was dark, with only a sliver of moonlight filtering through the curtains. As he moved toward the bed, he gently laid her down. Allowing himself to gaze down at her.

Her ebony hair pooled around her shoulders and spread out against the bed.

More. He wanted more. Pulling his shirt over his head, he planned to do this right. Take his time loving her body.

A gasp from her had him pausing.

"You glow?" she asked.

Deo looked down. His markings were mostly on his torso, less conspicuous than some of his brothers. "My markings glow from emotion and power. You, my dear mate, are my emotion."

He lowered himself, bracing above her.

"You are fascinating," she said, running a finger absently down his markings. A shiver ran down his spine at her touch.

Her fingers traced his skin. The more she touched, the

brighter they glowed. Lifting her head off the bed, she kissed him.

"I don't understand you, dragon shifter, but I'm willing to see where this goes."

His dragon purred as Deo kissed a trail down her body, pushing aside the cotton of her shirt as he worshiped her body one inch at a time until he was between her bare thighs.

Running his hands down her body, he clutched her thighs and licked the soft bud between her legs, down her slit.

She arched into him.

"Take off your pants," she moaned.

"Eager, aren't we?"

She wiggled her hips. "You're the one going off on the soul mates crap. So soul mate me already."

A heat pooled in his belly, hitting him straight between the legs. His dick strained against his jeans. Yeah. Maybe she had a point, and who was he to deny his mate.

He stood up and pulled at the waistband of his half-fastened pants. Shoving them down his hips, the strain of his hard-on freed.

The rapid beat of Aisha's heart called to him. She felt more than perhaps she let on.

Climbing over her, he slid his thigh between her own. His knee rubbing against her core. She let out a low moan as she rubbed against him.

"Ready for more already?"

Her voice breathy as she spoke. "Yes, more of you."

Shifting his weight, he pushed her thighs wide and positioned himself between them. Kissing her, he waited for the scent of her arousal to reach him, waited for her to tell him she wanted him like he wanted her.

Her hands slid up his arms, her nails running across his shoulder blades. The more she touched him, the brighter his markings glowed. Capturing her eyes with his own as he pulled away from her delicious mouth, whispering, "mine."

Her pelvis pushed against his dick, throbbing with restraint. "Yes, Deo. Yours."

Sliding his hand down over her beautiful curves and soft skin, he slid his fingers between her folds. Her hips pressed down against his fingers as he teased her, waiting for her juices to coat his hand.

She was ready. His dragon roared in desperate need to claim their mate. Not. Yet. Not. Yet.

The scent of her overwhelmed him and he thrust forward, pushing himself deep within her, his breath hissing through clenched teeth.

This was as much as she was ready to give, and he wouldn't push her.

Desperate to find a quenching of his own needs, he tried to keep this moment soft, slow. He tried to move over her in a gentle dance, but she took it away from him as she hooked her ankles behind his knees and shoved his shoulders.

Deo complied and watched as her breasts bounced as he rolled over with her seated on top of him. She rolled her hips, matching their previous pace. His head lolled back as she rode him.

Fuck, this felt good.

As he looked up through half-lidded eyes, his goddess rode him harder. His hands gripped her hips, helping her, pressing her against him harder, more.

7

$\mathcal{H}$er breathing came out ragged as she lost herself. Aisha tried to bite back her own cries as she rode Deo, moving herself toward an edge she'd only just learned existed. The need began to pulse within her, coming to the surface the faster she moved.

She'd never felt such need. A need to take what he offered. The need to not only rise toe to toe with the invisible edge, but to jump off. God, she needed this. Needed him.

Before that last thought could scare her, the waves of pleasure rose to a peak, and she cried out as her body exploded in a myriad of sensations. Her muscles quaked and pulled at Deo as he forced her to go over the edge and keep going until he thrust up, releasing his own need and spilling into her.

Her body responded again in an aftershock of more, as if it wanted to continue to give to him and take from him. God, she wanted to take whatever he gave her.

As the waves of her orgasm subsided, the pulse of Deo's dick within her slowed and she came down from a strange new high. Every nerve in her body was alive. She grabbed her own breasts and kneaded, moaning at the sensations. The muscles between her thighs pulsed, still trying to calm after the storm of pleasure.

"Oh, my God," she said on a breath.

Laying forward, her sensitive nipples rubbing against the hot skin of Deo's chest nearly brought her to the edge again. She licked her lips as she traced one of his markings. His tattoos still glowed, maybe brighter than before. She didn't care. They were beautiful. He was beautiful and for some unknown reason this god wanted her.

His powerful arms wrapped around her and held her in place, holding her safe.

This is what she'd wanted her entire life. No, not this exactly. The feeling she fit in somewhere was, though. Being a half-breed in the witch community was still judged. Sure, some said they accepted it, but so many looked down on her. Maybe that had been the drive for her to leave home. Find a more progressive group of witches and humans.

Deo didn't seem to care what she was. He just wanted her.

Even Tan didn't really get her. He was kind, supportive, and a good partner, but he didn't truly understand her witch side. He understood her desire to solve world suffering one research project at a time, but he didn't understand her need to embrace the magic flowing within her as well. He also didn't ignite a spark within her that had every cell in her body firing and coming to life.

She needed to stop going down this road. Thinking of another man while being here with Deo. But Tan had been her father's choice. Her father had asked her to take care of him. Really, it was his way of telling her to allow herself to be taken care of. Would Deo be that man? Would he take care of her?

A contented moan of pleasure escaping her own lips said yes.

"What are you thinking of, mate?"

She shook her head.

"Why do you call me that? You said you would have to bite

me, and I am sure even with all this." She motioned to them. "That I would have noticed."

His fingers traced small circles around her back, chasing shivers over her skin.

"Yes. You would notice, but not because it would hurt. You would feel more. But, mark or no mark, you are still mine. I will not mark you until you agree."

She began to sit up, pausing as his massive length pressed against her just so, causing her already sensitive muscles to nearly come again. Biting her lower lip, she tried to suppress more gasps of pleasure from escaping her. She couldn't help but wiggle against him, enjoying his reaction.

If she were smart, she'd sell her soul to him right now. Hell. She'd never come like this ever again, not with anyone else. She even struggled to figure out her own damn body with a vibrator. He'd ruined her, and she was all too happy to sign her life over to this dragon.

Lowering herself back down, her chest laying against his warmth, she waited for her body to calm itself again.

"What would convince you, mate?" he asked.

She couldn't think as his hands feathered up and down her sides. She didn't even know there were nerves on her sides. What had he asked? How could she think like this? Still in her, his hands doing things that didn't even seem possible, her body betrayed her and responded to every slight touch he offered.

What did she need? That's what he asked. Could she answer she needed a few more orgasms? No. that might actually kill her, maybe. But, damn. What a way to go.

"I just need time. I think. I'm getting there. I don't understand how you just know I'm meant for you. But, then again, maybe I just don't know how to listen. Is it your animal instincts? As a witch and human, I don't have that." She paused as she listened to his heartbeat under her ear.

It calmed even the deepest fear within her and she found

herself growing tired, at peace. Maybe she should sleep on it, or rather on him. No one made good choices when you were tired.

No, no one made good choices when tired and all your desires had been sated in one night. Then again, how could this turn out bad?

Aisha woke to the morning sun streaming in. As she moved, her body ached and slowly she remembered why. A weight had lifted from her chest and although she was sore, everything felt new.

Her eyes flew open. Was he still here? Reaching out across the bed she expected to find him, but no. Turning her head, she saw his rumpled side of the bed, but no Deo.

Sitting up, she tried to see if his clothes were still here? Maybe he was in the bathroom? But everything was silent. He left her?

Flopping down on the bed, Aisha closed her eyes. Her body ached from finally being used the way it was intended, but her heart ached from something very different. She would not let any more tears enter her life. So he'd left. He claimed she was his mate, that means he wouldn't have abandoned her. Still. He'd left.

Her nerves jumped at the unexpected squeak of the front door. She couldn't decide if it was Tan, in which case she should scramble for clothing.

"Tan?" she called out.

She pushed aside a sheet and started to look around for shorts and a T-shirt she usually left at the foot of the bed. Her bed didn't look anything like it usually did, not after Deo.

Without noticing, she'd squeezed her hands into fists and the bite of her fingernails waking her up a bit more. What the hell? He didn't come across as a one-night stand. A man did not profess soul deep need and then leave, unless you were claiming to be a dragon shifter and what if he wasn't?

"Don't come up. I'll be right down," she called out. That was all she needed. Tan to see her and her morning of shame. Toe curling, fantasy satisfying shame. But still. Not that she cared. Maybe she did.

One thing that was different and needed to stay that way was the conversation with Tan. She couldn't go back.

As she moved, her thighs twinged and a delicious pain of her well-used muscles between her legs reminded her just how much she couldn't go back to what her life was yesterday morning.

She also smiled at the thought that even now she'd probably let Deo claim her if he continued to do these things to her body. The man was hung. Like holy shit, that-isn't-going-to-fit kind of hung.

A giggle escaped. Had she stopped to think about what she'd been doing, she might have questioned how he was going to fit her. Luckily though, she was horny, and something in her needed him beyond all logic.

The bed rocked as she flopped back.

The cool air of her room brushed over her bare skin, eliciting a tiny shiver. He woke her up.

Memories of last night, before he'd done exactly as she'd secretly wanted, made her think about how things could have been different. She'd really tried to let him leave last night, but as she'd closed the door, her heart nearly broke. It felt like an elephant had sat on her chest and she couldn't breathe. If he left, the air would leave with him.

The moment she opened the door, no, the moment he came back to her, the peace he gave her settled in. The moment her hands were around him, the pain left her and all that was left was her soul deep need for a man she hadn't even known existed a few days ago.

Tan was just going to have to wait. Licking her lips, she wanted to relieve the burn of her dormant muscles somehow stretching for him as he'd pushed into her. Aisha moaned as her hand traveled down her body. Even just thinking about him made her need him all over again.

No. She didn't need him. She just lusted after him. But then what was the stabbing pain in the center of her chest. Why was it that if she didn't focus on the heat swirling in her belly, she could literally feel her heart shattering into a million little pieces.

Oh, right. He'd left her.

Someone cleared their throat, and she squeaked in surprise. Her hands grabbed at the sheets as she struggled to cover herself.

"Tan," she yelled, and then looked up.

No, it wasn't Tan. Deo had cleared his throat. A flurry of butterflies replaced the sludgy sadness.

"Should I put this down and come help?" He cocked a brow as his orangish eyes swirled into the blue of his dragon. Her skin tingled as they scanned down her body, leaving her bare and not just because she was naked.

Slipping her hands up and out of the sheets, she swallowed her embarrassment. Why she was she embarrassed when he'd already seen every inch of her?

"I…" what had he asked? She sniffed the air and the delicious scent of coffee filled her nose.

"Oh. Did you bring food?" she asked.

Finally taking in what was in his hands, she felt horrible for assuming he would leave her. She should have known better.

"Where did you get that?" Her stomach rumbled, and she stifled a smile as he stood a little taller.

"I have found a place with some oddly shaped woman with two tails. My brothers enjoy the coffee there. It keeps them a little less grumpy as this trip grows longer."

She perked up.

"Trip? You aren't from a local pack or whatever dragons belong to?"

He tilted his head, but continued to put a bag down.

"We aren't from around here. My brothers and I are warriors from another galaxy. We belong to a legion."

He sat down, and the bed dipped under his weight.

"What type of coffee would you like? I brought several flavors suggested by the adolescent female. I personally have decided these hazelnut lattes are delicious."

Studying the cups, she turned each one in the drink holder.

"This one." She pointed to a cup with something that looked to be caramel.

Pulling it from the tray, he handed it to her.

"Here are several items from their bakery. Whatever you would like."

Aisha's stomach growled again as if it were having its own conversation with the food. Grasping her stomach, she peeked in the bag.

"If you are hungry, eat. I can cook as well, but I don't think I'm very good, honestly."

Pulling out a sandwich, she smiled.

"No need. This is perfect. So now that we've uh, you know. Maybe it's time you explain things to me about you. Like, where are you from?"

8

"So let me get this straight. Aliens are real, and they aren't green creepy dudes with enormous eyes? They're hot dragons with bodies like gods and the ability to, well yeah," Aisha said.

Deo nodded. If he was following her words it sounded as if it all made sense. She was understanding his meaning.

"Yes, although not all aliens would look like me," he answered.

Aisha held her coffee cradled between her hands. Deo had hoped this discussion would be shorter and he could get back to pleasing her. He wasn't that selfless, his own dick wouldn't be complaining. Instead, she played a game of one million questions.

"Right. I get that, but my alien does look like a god. And you said you change into a dragon which, I mean, is hot."

Hot? He hadn't blown any fire around her. That would have been embarrassing. Or, well, it would be if he wasn't trying. This would be another language barrier, he thought. He was very good at languages, but after learning their information on the humans was out of date, he assumed there was also a lot of outdated language. Command would hear about this, someday.

"What does hot mean? Other than you mean hot as in heat like the sun or fire?"

Aisha tilted her head. "Hm. Well, you are hotter than any human man I can think of heat-wise. I mean you're hot, like when I look at you my panties are practically wet before you've even touched me."

Deo followed her movements as she put the coffee on the small table next to the bed. Slowly she stood up, the sheet she'd cradled for the last few minutes slipping away. Deo's nose flared at the scent of her.

Her legs straddled him as she settled on his lap.

The sweet aroma of arousal stirred his dragon and his dick.

"Hot means that you are good-looking. Beyond good-looking. You're like walking sex."

Odd words. Walking sex? He didn't even bother asking. Instead, he went with the one language he couldn't fuck up. He traced a hand up her thigh, his thumb grazing her heat as he stopped.

Her breath hitched and the scent of her need grew stronger.

"You are hot, my Aisha," he whispered before claiming her lush mouth.

Distracted by his kiss, he teased her, running the backs of his fingers over her heat and slipping one digit between her folds to her slick entrance. The gasp against his mouth, a satisfying reaction. Yes, he couldn't fuck this up.

His finger slid into her. Goddess, she was so wet. He stroked her, taking advantage of her legs spread wide on his lap. He was not letting this opportunity go.

Her breathing began to stutter against his mouth, and she broke the kiss to gasp in air.

He slipped in a second finger and started to stroke the sensitive spot that brought her the most pleasure.

"Deo-" she panted.

He smirked. "Yes, mate?"

She swallowed as her fingers dug into his shoulders.

"I want you," she breathed out, throwing her head back with a cry of pleasure.

His own need rolled through him as he watched her breasts tighten and her face flush pink. He needed her now.

Pulling out his fingers, he wrapped an arm around her back and stood, turning them around and laying her on the bed. He shoved off his pants in one quick motion.

He didn't wait for her to catch her breath, he couldn't wait for her. Her body called to him. He dipped his fingers into her once more and pulled them out, slicking his erection with her juices.

Gripping her legs, he pulled her to the edge of the bed in one quick motion. Leaning in, he claimed one taut peak of her breast as he pushed into her, stretching her, making her moan.

He pumped in and out as he nibbled one nub and then the other before he moved to her sweet mouth to swallow her next cry of desire. As his own desperate desire to mark her grew, he had to fight against his dragon, heightening his own desperation.

His frustration of denying his most basic need driving him to thrust into her harder and harder, fighting against his soul deep need.

He couldn't claim her, not yet. Instead, he slammed into her over and over, feeling the waves of her core begin to milk him, pull from him and her cries growing desperate and yet still she would take more. She had to.

He couldn't help his own need for her, he couldn't quench his desperation to claim her as his, but he needed to try.

"Deo. Oh, God. Deo," she cried.

Her voice brought on his orgasm as he slammed into her one more time as her muscles pulsed again around him. He spilled into her as he thrust one last time.

As his dick slowly stopped pulsing within her, he reached for her and held her, rolling over so she was on top again.

They lay there for a few minutes. His heart beating to match the rhythm of hers.

"Wow," she said, after her breathing returned to normal.

He stroked her hair. "Are you okay?" he asked.

Her cheek slid across his chest as she gave a slow nod. "I think so."

Deo paused a moment and wondered if he'd hurt her and she wasn't being honest. This wasn't going well. He thought tasting her would be enough, and now, well he wasn't sure he was strong enough to fight fate's plan.

"Are you sure?"

She lifted her head, resting a chin on his chest. "Yes. I mean. Wow, that was intense, but good Lord, yes. I am fine. I may not be walking anywhere for awhile, mind you."

A smile crossed her lips.

"I am resisting instinct by not claiming you mate. You are infuriating and also beyond enticing. I can't deny you your wishes."

An idea came to him as he said those last words. How could he gain her full trust, her permission, and her love? Perhaps by combining her love of science for her curiosity of his world. Perhaps she could accomplish everything she needed to fully give herself to him and their fated life.

"Aisha," he said, pushing back a stray hair crossing her forehead.

"Hmm?" she answered, her eyes closing.

"What if I showed you my lab on the ship?"

Her eyes opened, and he watched as her expression changed from sleepy contentment to curiosity.

"Your lab?" she asked.

He nodded and rolled them over to their sides. Pulling out as she protested, he laughed.

"I can't think with you naked, woman. You've asked for me to prove myself and I want to. So, what do you say about seeing my ship and the lab that would be at your disposal?"

Deo stood up. "You will need clothing, something somewhat warm."

Pushing herself up, she rolled her eyes. "Indulge me. Why?"

"Just meet me out back."

He turned to head downstairs and stopped.

"Have you flown before?"

Her answer was guarded. "Yes."

"Should I assume it was in some kind of mechanical device? A ship of some sort?" he asked.

"Where is this going, Deo?"

"I wanted your permission to fly you to the ship." He watched her eyes grow wider in realization.

"Like as a dragon?" she asked.

His dragon started to surface, he scratched at his forearms as his dragon damn near pushed his way out. Anything to stretch their wings.

"Yes. As a dragon."

Aisha stood up and closed the gap between them, touching the skin he scratched.

"Is this, well, this isn't human skin. Your dragon?"

Deo looked down. He'd never had to restrain himself like this before so he'd never noticed just how his dragon appeared at different times within the shift.

The blue of his scales covered his arms. Things one never thought about.

"Yes. This is my dragon skin. I have many forms before I fully shift."

She smiled. "Fascinating from a science standpoint. Nothing about you makes sense." She snorted. "Well, not that shifters make sense at all. It's magic, I suppose, not physics."

Science, this was a language he preferred as well, but there was little to explain when it came to his dragon form. "Yes. It is magic, not physics, unfortunately. The goddess blessed those who she deemed worthy of being a warrior before we were born. We are the chosen. I assume other shifters are this way as well?"

Aisha shrugged. "There isn't really any research. I mean, maybe there is, but I don't think it is done with common knowledge. Just like witches and fae. I guess that's why I'm always studying demonology. I think there is a tie between all of us. What we are comes from ancient magics mixed into the human race. I think."

This fascinated him, that her people did not understand who they were or where they came from. He never had to wonder about his origins. He knew, as did his father before him.

"I have heard that demons have been the source of many things throughout the centuries. It also proves the other realms and worlds could be responsible for all that is possible here on Earth. But I do not question my existence as you do. I know my place. Perhaps you have not found yours, yet?"

He liked the way she studied his dragon, the way his dragon calmed for a moment at the touch of their mate.

She stroked the skin. "It's just fascinating. I know sometimes I have to accept that there aren't always answers. But I'm not there. I believe cancer can be cured like so many other diseases. I believe there is a reason why I am who I am. I still believe that maybe supernatural blood is the cure for human suffering and I'm not ready to let that go. I think this has always been my purpose."

Deo wanted to hold her and make all her worries disappear, but he had a feeling that her mission, her convictions were what made Aisha his Aisha.

"I understand. I want to help you find your answers. Let me fly you to my lab?"

She pursed her lips for a moment before releasing his arm.

"So what you are saying is I get to ride you?"

Deo nodded. This was logical, yes.

Her face reddened as her body shook before a loud burst of

laughter came out.

"Oh my. You are so deadpan serious and all I can think of is how, I mean, well when we, in the bedroom and I... Well, I mean, I was on top. And now, you say I get to ride your dragon. My mind is not at all being mature about this."

Deo's own eyes widened at what she was referring to and even he had a hard time not laughing. He knew good and well what it was like to have her on top of him. His dick was already rising to the occasion. Fuck. He needed to not go there. He'd already nearly lost his control before.

The idea that she thought that about his dragon was rather humorous and physically not possible. She'd soon see. At least laughter was much easier than skepticism and fear. It was easier than the frustrations of not claiming her.

"Then it is agreed. You will allow me to take you to my ship." He headed for the backyard, the only place he could think to be inconspicuous. Most people would notice a large dragon in the front yard he supposed.

He paused again, just outside the door. "Aisha?"

She looked up from a drawer she'd grabbed a shirt from.

"It would be my pleasure to let you ride me in any form, mate." He winked as her mouth fell open.

"Meet me outside," he called back.

That was funny, he thought to himself. Deo was proud of himself. This human humor thing was becoming more and more natural.

Outside he waited. His dragon's tail thwacking against the spotty grass yard. They hated to wait, and his dragon was growing impatient. Deo scolded the damn beast that this wasn't the time for them to show off. Only, his dragon scoffed at that idea. Of course he did.

A bird landed a few feet away and his dragon's head snapped up. Things just got interesting. Deo didn't care that he was part of the animal, when instinct took control things never went as planned. The dragon snuck up on the bird, slowly crawling on his belly.

Well, at least it kept him from getting impatient and trying to stir up trouble with the neighbor's dog.

He crawled forward, slower as he got on the tail feathers of the bird. Once they were right behind the oblivious creature, he blew air out of his snout and scared the tiny thing. His dragon was just about ready to take off after it, when it caught the scent of Aisha and heard a feminine sigh.

"I wanted to tell you how impressed I was at the dragon, because well it's obviously you, Deo but really?"

The dragon turned around and sat on his haunches, his tongue lolling out of the side of his mouth. Deo wanted to roll his eyes at the pathetic display, but deep down he too just wanted to be near their mate.

"I really thought you'd be more scary," Aisha said.

His dragon smiled.

"Oh. Never mind. I. Yeah. Don't do that."

His dragon stood on all fours and moved closer to her. Communication would be much easier if they were mated. Which obviously wasn't going to happen this time around.

"How do we do this? Me, getting on?" she asked.

Deo had his dragon lower himself and put a leg out, hoping she'd use that to boost her up.

Aisha tilted her head and then shrugged. Walking forward, she put a foot on his arm and scrambled up his side.

His dragon twisted around, trying to see that she was safe.

"Okay. Giddy up?"

His dragon's chest rumbled with laughter as he took off into the sky.

ell, there was no time like the present to get an MRI.

Her hair was windblown, and this was a ship. All right. This was real. Probably. Deo had offered her the chance to see a lab with more technology than she could imagine, and yet she hadn't actually believed him. Because you know. Aliens.

Right. Maybe she should have started drinking before she got on the dragon. Ha. She laughed at the whole idea. Like she needed to drink. She'd just ridden on a dragon.

What was a bigger deal? Dragon or ship? Dragon or ship? Tough choices. Should she call her therapist? No. Two outcomes and neither sounded good. Either the therapist would believe her and call this in to the government, or the more likely option is she would call her nuts and push more pills and maybe a new stylish straight jacket.

"I'm on a spaceship? Like an actual ship that goes up there?" She pointed up. Deo eyed her kind of funny. Okay, maybe she was acting a little strange. He had told her the truth. Only, until this moment she'd thought he was using metaphors or something. I mean, spaceship. Sure. Okay. And alien. And a dragon.

But one never actually believes anything until you're standing in the entrance of said ship. Or maybe she was still in denial of a dragon. Aisha had thought Deo as a human was hot, but in his dragon form. Well, hell, it wasn't legal to think of an animal that way. But seriously. All that raw power. Maybe it was just that it was Deo under the powerful blue beast. A sexy, godlike man that could make her wet by a simple look. She'd have jumped his very naked ass right now, except well. Spaceship.

"What do you think?" he asked, as they started down a hallway.

Think. Did one think about the interior design of a spaceship?

"Rustic?" That was all that came to mind. What had she expected? A saucer maybe? This appeared pretty roomy and looked more like an aerodynamic camper or something. Really, it didn't make any sense.

"My lab's down this way."

Her feet moved, but her brain was on vacation right now. A moment in curiosity got the better of her. "What is that?" she asked.

Deo looked over his shoulder. That's what you call a kitchen, but really, it's our common area.

She nodded.

A few more feet and another door.

"What is in there?"

Deo shook his head. "Would you like a tour first?"

She couldn't nod her head fast enough.

"You will soon enough know the ship, so if this makes you happy, I will show you."

It made her happy, or at least took the edge off of her crazy. This was nuts. Seriously. She was on a spaceship. They walked into what he called the kitchen. But truly it was large enough for a cafeteria? Spacious.

"How many of them are there?" she asked.

He glanced back, a hint of a smile as his eyes went from man to dragon. "Dragons, you mean?"

Aisha nodded. She wasn't there yet, saying the words.

He shrugged. "On this ship there are six of us. We are the ones who need mates but have yet to find them. There are more of us, some mated. Some still young enough they do not need a mate yet. They remain back home."

She nibbled on her lower lip as he walked across the room to a small area of shelves. Damn, he was good looking and knowing what he could do to her just made him that much better.

The lights were low, but she saw him sliding fabric over a leg. Pants. Well, dang it. She was really enjoying this view.

She let out an audible sigh. Probably for the best. It was a little odd to walk around naked, she figured, especially if they weren't alone. Now that she knew there were at least six, she assumed they weren't alone. Aisha knew at least one other had a mate, wife, whatever.

Yeah. No. Aisha didn't want another woman seeing him in all his glory. Because glorious it was.

Out through another doorway, he stopped and waited for her to follow.

"This is our briefing room, although for now we have made other uses of it."

Two women sat on the floor in a pile of pillows.

Aisha slid behind Deo as they jumped up from their places.

"Oh my gosh, is this her?"

Deo smiled. "Yes, Maddie. This is my Aisha."

Aisha caught her breath as Deo looked at her. The pride sparkling in his eyes eclipsed the lust that had filled them last night.

A woman came over and gave her a one-armed hug.

"Sorry. I know this is really strange. Like really strange. Good news though, you'll see a lot of Lilly and me."

A smaller woman waved, almost afraid to come from behind

Maddie. Aisha had some memory of the girl and how afraid of everything she was, except with that other huge guy around.

"Sorry. I'm Maddie, like Deo said. This is Lilly." She looked around Deo at Aisha. "Are you moving in now? Did you bring anything?"

The wheels began to turn. Lilly was with the other man she'd met at her office a week ago. But who was Maddie with? Deo would most definitely be able to please more than just Aisha, but that would not work for her. He was hers.

Her heart stopped. Or rather it probably didn't, but she sure as hell thought the world had stopped. At what point exactly did she start to think of Deo as hers? Sure she'd told him what he wanted to hear during sex, because at that point literally he could have done anything, and she would have been fine with it. Literally anything.

But right now. Right now, this odd tightness in her chest at the thought he might want someone else made her stomach churn. She was jealous.

Oh, no. She wasn't there yet. Was she? Maybe she was.

Maybe it was time to jump ship. Or maybe it was time for something else. Or, well, shit.

"Aisha? So are you? Moving in? Be prepared to be overprotected that's for sure," Maddie smiled.

"Um, Maddie, was it?" Aisha asked.

Maddie nodded. "I know Lilly is with that big guy that came to my lab, but I assume you have a mate as well the way you just said that?"

She grabbed Deo's arm, as if that staked her claim. But, yeah. No one was touching him.

Wonderful first impression. Jealousy.

Crap on a cracker. She hadn't been jealous of anyone since like the third grade when her crush preferred a normal girl who didn't accidentally turn her pencil into a snake. To be fair, Aisha sort of preferred that too. Maybe that was why Tan had been an appealing agreement.

He was normal and safe, and she was trying to be normal. Most days. Unless it came to her research. That was how she seemed to get the need for magic out of her system, in her lab.

Maddie was practically bouncing. "Oh, my mate is Kal. I don't know if you've met him." She was quiet for a second.

"Yeah, no he says he hasn't, but he's coming now."

Lilly peeked around Maddie and finally came into full view.

"You're the scientist? Did you ever figure out my blood?" Lilly asked, wringing her hands.

The high of knowing Deo was not a man whore, or not trying to have his own little harem was a relief. What the hell would she have done had he wanted her to share? She'd have smacked someone, that's what would have happened.

Oh, God. She was seriously beyond lust right now. She wanted him, like wanted him, wanted him. Like that whole word 'mine' he'd said finally meant something to her. He was hers, just as she was his. No. Not yet. No wait. Maybe yes? Wow. This was confusing.

"Brother, I hear you finally brought your mate to meet us?"

Aisha turned to the voice behind her.

Deo did an odd handshake thing and then turned back to pull her forward.

Wow. Big. So big. Were they all this big? Damn their planet had a superpower breeding men.

"You must be Aisha. Deo has talked nonstop about you. We've been all hoping he would bring you by soon enough."

Words. She needed to speak words. What kind of words? She was super smart and yet at this moment freaking out about her feelings took over all logic.

"Hi. Yes." Those were words that answered some questions. Maybe not his questions, but someone's somewhere.

She watched as Kal sidestepped her and embraced Maddie.

Aisha's eyes took it all in. The way he held her, kissed her, cared for her.

"Brother, I hear we have another female to liven the place up?"

Another man, this one familiar. Why did he look so much more scary here, when he was smiling?

"I'm Eadric. Do you remember me?"

A nod was all she managed.

Her lungs hurt. She couldn't get a deep breath. She was supposed to see a lab. And a ship. Not suddenly figure out her entire world made sense, and she was supposed to give everything up for this man.

Looking up, he caught her eyes at the same time. Like he knew her already.

"Brothers? Maddie, Lilly. Please excuse me as I give Aisha the remaining tour."

No one protested or seemed to notice her gasping.

She couldn't get a deep breath. What was wrong with her? As they walked she finally got relief, only for her lungs to protest again.

Holding her hand to her heart she felt the darn thing beating like a determined little drummer. Only hers was trying to beat its way out of her chest.

"Aisha. Calm yourself. Are you okay?"

She started to nod, only to turn the motion into a shake.

"I'm sorry," she said, her words winded.

"Come, let me help you."

He lifted her and quickened his pace down a long hallway.

She didn't care where they went. She couldn't protest, anyway. This was a panic attack. It finally dawned on her. She had them under control. Aisha had been fine for like a month or two. No, she hadn't. She'd simply learned to turn off the part of her that felt just like she did growing up when she scared human kids or was rejected by magical kids.

No.

Right now she didn't recognize this world, her world, and it scared her. She wasn't a robot. She couldn't pretend anymore. But that also meant she had to realize something else. Could she? Could she risk having someone else to lose? Someone she could love?

A swoosh sound brought her down from the spiral of panic. Deo walked into a darkened space. As he put her down on a soft surface, Aisha realized it was a bed.

"Is this your room?"

Aisha held her hand to her chest as she tried to focus on breathing.

A light turned on, revealing Deo by a side table.

"Aisha, would you tell me what's wrong?"

Breathing. That's what was wrong. She couldn't get in enough air. Her chest burned and her heart raced. She couldn't shake the feeling that something was wrong.

"I'm just panicking. That's all."

He took a seat next to her.

"Panicking over what?" he asked.

Aisha didn't know where to start.

"Everything. Your brothers and their mates. They looked so happy," she said.

Happy was an understatement. The moment Eadric had entered the room, Lilly changed. She looked as if the world was right, finally. She was changed from even the last time Aisha had seen her, terrified in a chair. Even then, Eadric had been the one to calm her.

None of that was really the issue, though.

The issue was that she was falling for Deo. She wanted what those two women had. No, she wanted what Deo and she were only just starting to have. But how did she tell him she was falling for him? She wasn't ready. She wasn't ready to be claimed, or mated, or whatever. She wasn't ready to abandon her life goal.

She wasn't ready to let go of the feeling she was finally onto something.

But everything she thought she might be onto was a dead end. Always. Deo though, he was something else. She'd never felt this way before. She tried to slow her breathing and thought about the way her body seemed to find a new calm whenever he touched her. The way everything seemed to melt away into the background when he looked at her. She focused on the way her body woke up, feeling something and everything whenever he kissed her.

He shifted on the bed. Taking her face in-between his hand, he held her attention.

"I cannot fix what I don't know, Aisha. Tell me and I will fix it."

10

A rock sat in the pit of Deo's stomach. If his mate was not happy, he couldn't be. He didn't need to be connected to her to know that there was some kind of war within her and he wasn't allowed to fix it.

He growled.

Why wouldn't she let him? This is what mates did. This is what he did. He fixed.

"Aisha. Let me help you."

She closed her eyes for a moment. He could feel the tick of every passing second.

"I feel this pull toward you. You're right. I don't know how to say no to it. I want to be near you. But there is the other part of me. The side of me that can't let go of my pain. The fact so many others have to lose someone. But as a shifter, I'm sure you don't get that. I've studied some of their blood and I can't figure out why you are immune to so much."

Deo heard her words. If he could stop the world from suffering, he would. Wouldn't anyone with a heart? He wished he could find the secret. All the innocent lives lost in senseless wars, all

73

playing on the frailty of this species. It was all too much to understand the why. Aisha needed to understand that maybe, at some point, it wasn't her destiny to find all the answers.

"Aisha. It's not all on you to save everyone from pain. You can't. If Earth is anything like the many other planets in the universe, hundreds and sometimes thousands are trying to find the answer and cures to things that plague their populations. Sometimes you can't and sometimes all you can do is contribute. Offer. Maybe you've stumbled onto something that someone else could use?"

Deo released her face as her eyes watered.

"What is that supposed to mean?"

He ran his tongue over his teeth. This felt a lot like walking a very thin line over a pit of death. If he'd said something wrong, he didn't mean to, but the way she glared at him said he'd done something far worse.

"I just meant that maybe it's time for you to move on. Find a fresh perspective? I can offer-"

She cut him off. "You're suggesting giving up years of research for what? To screw you? To sit and watch movies all day while you go out and do what? What do those women do all day? Anything?"

Yup. He'd fucked this up. "I'm sorry. I didn't mean to upset you. I was merely offering to help you, perhaps offer some new resources that my planet has. One of my brothers is more the scientist and could-"

"I've listened to what I can and can't do my entire life. I've been told what I am and am not. Don't. Just don't tell me."

Deo removed himself from the bed and stood.

That wasn't what he had been trying to do. He thought he was being supportive. Deo had meant that the world wasn't sitting on her shoulders, because he knew that feeling. He knew what going into battle felt like and knowing the second a warrior was down, and their life would depend on his speed and accuracy. And at that moment it felt like the world did indeed rest on his shoulders.

"Aisha, that was not what I meant."

He paced the room. He'd seen today going very differently.

"I am not telling you what to do." Only, maybe he had. He was getting a little desperate to earn her trust. He was also starting to struggle against his dragon. Every time she was near his skin rippled with the dragon's need for her. Desperation wasn't a good look for him. He needed to claim her, or at least get a taste of her again. His resolve faltering. A lot.

"What do you want from me? I would give you anything to make you happy," he asked.

She looked up at him. "I want to go home."

He wouldn't allow her to see the hurt, but the stabbing within his chest was almost enough to have him down on his knees.

No. This was not what he had wanted. Somehow, though, he felt like if he didn't return her home, the trust he was working so hard to gain would be lost for good.

"Yes. Of course. I'll take you home."

He held his hand out and was relieved when she took it. Perhaps this was a slight hiccup, like Kal and the chicken incident, or Eadric and the antidote. Or like when he first met Aisha and asked her for help, and he had to do everything he could to not mark her then. For him, he'd been pining away for his mate since he'd first caught her scent mixed with that of chemicals of her lab. But for her, a witch or human, she was only starting to feel the effects of finding her mate.

He could and would ensure that she trusted him, even if that took a few more days. He hoped.

Guiding her out of the ship, he continued to glance back. She wouldn't look up. She fidgeted, chewed her lip, and at one point whiped away what he assumed were tears.

His tongue a sandpaper desert every time he thought to speak. He'd even reached out to his brothers who sent back little help, more confusion, and sadness. Not a single fucking male in his life knew what to say to fix anything with these females.

Great.

As they left the ship he stopped. "Aisha, I would never keep you from your work. Whatever you need or want, I will make sure you get." He gave a gentle tug and when she didn't protest, he wrapped her in his arms. "I just need you. I will wait if that is what you need. I just need you."

She said nothing as he backed away, tossing the pants aside and letting his dragon slowly surface.

This time he waited to shift until she was paying attention. Her eyes widened and sparkled in fascination.

Standing tall, he let his dragon take over, unfurling his wings as he stretched into the freedom.

Show off, Deo thought to his damn dragon. Sometimes it was much easier to let this dumb beast take over. He seemed to miss all the small subtleties and focus only on the tasks at hand.

His dragon turned toward Aisha. Her steps were slow, but less cautious than earlier. His dragon bowed toward her and extended his leg. She patted his neck and although Deo was less satisfied that she appeared to like this dragon better than his human form, she at least wasn't running. Not that she could go far in the middle of nowhere.

Standing next to him, she laid her hand along his hide. His dragon's chest rumbled in contentment.

If only life were always this easy.

Deo's dragon craned his neck to the side; a reassuring snuff of the air all he could do.

The scent of sadness lingered as she climbed on and Deo didn't even really understand what had happened. Of course he didn't. But he would figure it out.

As she straddled his neck, the dragon wiggled his hide a bit to make sure she was secure, eliciting a slight laugh. Maybe all hope wasn't lost.

Turning around, he took a few steps and pushed off, catching the wind with his wings.

All things wrong in the world, and at least he still had the freedom of the sky.

Nothing could be wrong up here. Or maybe it could, but not right now. Aisha was with him, safe, and the world faded away below them.

Closing his eyes, he wished he could communicate with her right now. Let her know that he would take away her pain if he could. He'd do anything to allow her peace.

Deo soared in and out of a few white puffs in the sky, gaining an extra giggle here and there. It wasn't enough, nothing would be, not until she was safe in his arms forever.

A few minutes passed, the trip being much too quick as he circled her home, watching to make sure no one was on the street. Finding his opportunity, he quickly landed.

Aisha slid down, and he instantly shifted. He would not waste this moment. Every chance he had could be his last if he wasn't careful. Nothing was certain, even if it should have been, even if the goddess deemed this to be, it still wasn't certain.

"May I come in?" he asked.

She gave an audible sigh. "Can I just have some time?"

He nodded. Well, it was worth asking. "Of course. Would I be allowed to come back tonight?"

Her head tilted. "Uh. I mean, like a day of time? Come back tomorrow?"

Deo resisted the urge to rub the center of his chest, where his heart was currently being a baby and pumping pain through his body at the speed of lightning. He nodded. It wasn't what he had wanted. He wanted to fall asleep with his Aisha pressed against him. He wanted to fall asleep next to his mate after he had kissed away the sadness and confusion surrounding her.

"Yes. Whatever you need. Please, before I go though. Tell me what's wrong, mate? I would deny you nothing, you know that, right?"

Sucking on her bottom lip, she turned her eyes down.

"Honestly? I just don't know if I'm ready for all this."

She waved a hand between them.

The air was sucked out of his lungs. Ready for this? Did she mean that she was rejecting him? Was that even possible? No one had ever told him of an Amit warrior being rejected. What if she did? What then? Did he just wait for the dragon to overtake him?

Well, if he would cease to exist, what the hell did he have to lose. He moved forward and cupped the back of her head as he smashed his lips to hers.

This moment would remain his for eternity, even if he wasn't who he was now. He tasted her, flicking his tongue against hers. Exhaustion hit him. As a fixer by nature, he always had the answers. He was tired though. Right now, he only wanted to feel. Perhaps he couldn't fix her, convince her, or reason with her. He could give one last thing and that was himself.

If she didn't want him for what he was, then at least he'd gone out knowing he'd done his best. Letting down his people, his brothers wasn't ideal, but at least the others would find their mates. He was sure of it. They would pass on their bloodlines.

He grabbed her ass. Goddess, he wanted her, but he wouldn't. He would walk away and come back tomorrow for what he feared would be the last judgment. But perhaps she would see reason and follow her heart. It was up to the goddess now.

Deo gave her one last kiss and then pulled away. His hard shaft would be difficult to ignore as he moved back, away from her. Yeah, this would fucking suck, but he had no choice.

Turning away from her, he shifted and mid stride took off

before he lost all control and his dragon overtook the logic. No one wanted a mate that wasn't willing.

He took one last glance down at her as they rose higher and higher into the sky.

She looked just as tortured as he felt.

11

She shielded her eyes as she watched him fly away. She couldn't breathe. Aisha wrapped her arms around her stomach, the stabbing pain of regret shooting through her. What had she done? Would he come back? Did she know how to get in touch with him?

This wasn't supposed to be like this. Her personal life. It wasn't supposed to be complicated.

Aisha had already dealt with complicated. She'd lost what mattered to her. She accepted that she would never really be accepted anywhere, and she accepted a marriage that was at its best agreeable. But right now. All that seemed stupid. What if she'd just lost the last thing that would really matter to her, something even more powerful than the love for her father?

The world started to close in around her. The air was too thick to breathe in. The gravity too strong to fight as she fell to the ground, her knees hitting the grass. She clutched at her shirt, gripping the fabric against her chest.

It hurt. Her heart literally hurt.

But she didn't want to be someone's to control, and she didn't want to give up her research. The one thing that had made her feel something after her father died. Something that had given her purpose. She'd never truly known her purpose until she'd found her research. But now?

She just wanted to be touched again, but by him. He brought back feeling within her. She was no longer numb, and she wasn't entirely sure that the human side of her could turn it off again.

Crap. What should she do?

Deep breaths. She needed to clear her head. This was just a panic attack. It was fine. She could be okay.

Her legs shook as she made her way to the back door. She would be okay. She would fix her mistakes.

Maybe. Yanking at the door, she nearly fell into the kitchen as she quickly scanned the room for her purse. It was here somewhere. The door slammed behind her and she turned her head back and forth. Her purse had to be here. She was sure of it.

There. Behind the chair on the floor. Someday she was going to get her shit together. Someday. Yanking it up, the purse thunked against the table.

Rifling around the disorganized interior, she couldn't find it. The card. Deo had given her a card with a number on it to call if she ever figured out the chip. She needed that number now.

Think. "Where the hell is it?" she asked no one. Closing her eyes, she tried to remember. He'd handed it to her, and she might have been a little distracted by his looks, but she'd taken it and, and what?

Oh right. She still had it back on her desk. Of course she did.

Shit. Okay.

She just needed to go back to the college. It was fine. Running through the house, she grabbed her keyring with her office key and went straight through the front door.

"Aisha? Where have you been?" called Tan.

She waved him off as she ran past him. "Can't talk. I'll be back."

"What?"

She didn't bother answering. Aisha ran as fast as her chubby little legs would go. At some point she would get in shape. Maybe today was that day because her damn thighs burned, and she needed to push through. She needed to fix this, now.

Doubling over at the corner, it was apparent this was not the day. Sucking in air like one of those fish that cleans the walls of a tank, she tried not to pass out. No. Today was not that day. Still, she needed to get to the college.

As the air caught up with her and her lungs stopped heaving, she stood up and power walked. At least she would arrive breathing almost normally.

A few blocks, and she was finally climbing the stairs to her office. Wonderful, so many wonderful crappy stairs.

God, this world had it in for her. She passed a few labs, the science department's main office, and finally got to her door. A man stood in front of of it studying the posted hours. She didn't have any office hours today, so why was he here?

"Can I help you?"

His lips formed a thin line, and she wasn't sure if it was meant to be a smile, but a shiver ran up her spine. Creepy guy alert.

"Yes. I believe you can."

She stood there, waiting. *Creepy dude, let's go, spit it out.*

"And?" she asked.

This time she was pretty sure it was a smile, that or gas as a corner of his mouth turned up.

"I believe you have something that belongs to me? A chip?"

Strange request for a chemistry department.

"I, uh. No. Maybe you should try the engineering department?"

He lifted a device.

"Well, I don't think I will need to. The chip has a tracker, and it suddenly started working again. Leading me here."

Deo brought her the chip, and he hadn't mentioned any creepy men. This guy didn't look like someone Deo would associate with. Everything within her was screaming to run. Only Aisha wasn't sure she could trust herself lately.

She'd just let Deo leave, thinking she didn't want him. No, thinking she couldn't handle him? Really, she just needed time. A few minutes of extreme soul crushing pain helped clear her mind. It wasn't every day that you suddenly realized you truly, without exception, love someone. Until a few days ago, she wasn't even sure she could feel again.

"Well, you must have a glitch then. I'm honestly not sure what you are talking about."

He studied her.

"Do you mind moving so I can get into my office at least?"

The gentleman moved aside, but Aisha wasn't sure she wanted to pass him. There was something off about him. He was pale, rail thin, and didn't appear to have any facial expressions.

She didn't trust people that didn't like food or people that looked like robots. He was both and that wasn't boding well for him right now.

Sidestepping him, giving him a quick glance to ensure he stayed put, she slid the key into her door. Aisha had hoped that he would leave, but as she pushed it open, he followed her in.

Pulling her phone out of her pocket, she unlocked it. Was this one of those moments you called emergency services, campus police, or the dragon?

Oh, right? She needed to find his number.

"Sorry. I've got some things to do. Could you come back for normal office hours and I will see if I can help track down what you think is here?"

She looked up, her skin crawling. He stood above her.

"Miss. I don't think you understand. We are willing to pay handsomely to get our property back."

Standing up slowly, Aisha was listening. Because, money.

"I'm still not sure I know that I have what you want."

He nodded. "Well, let me be clear we know you not only have

our chip, but you also have a creature, an alien, that turns into a dragon that also wanted the chip."

Aisha froze. This conversation was going south. Was it in her head that the room had just cooled five degrees?

"My client is willing to pay you enough to fund your department for years if you not only return our chip but also the dragon."

She froze. Who asked for a person, a living being, as if they weren't something that had feelings? He was talking about Deo, she was sure of that. Who the hell was he, anyway? She needed to find Deo's number, and now. Something wasn't right.

"I'm sorry. Who are you?"

His skeletal like face almost appeared to morph into what might have been emotion.

"Who I am is not a concern. What I can do for you is."

Aisha shook her head.

"I'm sorry. I can't help you. I don't know who you are talking about. And this chip? Again, I'll look. Come back tomorrow."

He pulled out a card.

"Here is my number. I will do as you ask. But keep this in mind. Is any one creature worth more than a lifetime of work?"

She paused.

"What do you mean?"

God, she needed to shut her mouth and get him to go away.

His thin bony fingers scratched at his nose, such a normal gesture for someone so freakishly not normal.

"What I mean is, what is one alien if we can supply you with enough funding you would never have to apply for another grant." He pointed at his card. "I've taken the liberty of writing the figure we had in mind. If you return the chip, we may consider additional funds."

Creepy man walked out, leaving a trail of what-the-fuck-had-just-happened.

But really. What had just happened? Opening her desk, she

took out a key and turned around to a fridge she kept in her tiny space. She kept the lock on it to keep people out of her yogurt stash, and because sometimes she broke a few rules on handling chemicals. This time it was the chip.

Peeking over her shoulder, she wanted to make sure he'd really gone. Thinking twice, she got up and closed her office door, clicking the lock in place just in case.

She chewed the inside of her cheek. Unlocking the fridge, she reached for a small petri dish.

Pulling out the dish that housed what she thought was a dormant chip, she gently laid it on her desk.

The day this little chip had come into her life brought more than just Deo. The strange signatures of Lilly's blood was one of them, and the odd residue that was most definitely a poison.

Knowing Lilly, seeing her timid and small, Aisha didn't even consider that what she suspected was true. But it was. Her blood had demonic properties. She was human, but she was also something not from this side of normal. Aisha snorted.

"Join the damn club," she mumbled.

Studying, she wanted to know what the man would want with it. Even if what he said was true. The chip held some familiar chemical residues, but there were also traces of elements that she couldn't identify.

Why would they want this back, and what were they doing poisoning people? Yeah, turning Deo over to a bunch of people who thought killing people was a good idea, didn't sound promising. If they wanted an alien, then they were obviously aware of them, and that gave her reason to pause. What were these people exactly? What was creepy guy? Not human?

She leaned back in her chair. None of this was a good sign. Years of grounding herself in science and here she was, believing that there was something else out there. If she didn't know about other realms, maybe this would be more strange. Demons existed. Of course the Fae existed. So maybe it was logical to think that aliens did as well.

Sighing, she put the chip down and her eye caught the paper with Deo's handwriting. She needed to call him. She needed to see him. She wouldn't sell him. He was a living person, and no one was worth a price. The chip, however. Maybe she could talk Deo into letting her exchange that? Flipping creepy guy's card over, her eyes bugged out.

That was a lot of zeros. So many. Damn, Deo was a catch apparently. Well, she knew that. But what would make him worth this much?

What she could do with that kind of money. She could start her own research facility, maybe even have a team of magically based chemists. She was certain that any cure would have to be a mix of human and magical compounds. She just hadn't figured them out yet.

She was so close though. A rat that should have died a year ago was still running around and somewhat healthy. She'd even named him Herbie, because she was convinced he would be around for a while more. But it didn't fix it all. Not by a long shot. This money, though. Wow.

No. She couldn't. She loved Deo for whatever reason unknown to her; he was what her heart desperately wanted. Even the thought of turning him over to someone made her skin crawl.

Shaking her head in amusement, she did somewhat wonder how they thought she'd turn him in, anyway. Good luck making him do anything.

Crap. She'd come here to tell him that. To tell him she loved him. Right? That's what she'd agreed with herself. She was fixing her mistake of sending him away.

It was probably in her head, but the air grew thicker as she tried to breathe. Yeah. She needed to call. She was falling apart without him. She just needed to figure out what to do with her life after that.

If she told him she loved him, what would happen? Maybe she could take her research with her? He said he had access to labs. He'd mentioned other science minded people, well probably dragons. And maybe her issue was she needed more perspective. Could you get more perspective than being light years away?

Okay. So maybe there were still a lot of questions.

Grabbing the chip, she carefully put it in her satchel hung over the back of her chair. Grabbing his number and her phone, she headed back out, locking her door as she left.

Aisha dialed the number to Deo's phone as she walked. Her body maneuvered on autopilot as she waited for him to answer.

Before she knew it she was outside. Nothing seemed like it had before, not now. Not since she'd met Deo and then pushed him away.

There was no answer.

"Damn it."

Pulling the phone away, the screen was dark. Not even the chance to leave a voicemail.

"Fine. I'll just keep calling. We'll see who is more stubborn." She punched at the redial as if waging war on the phone. Okay, it wasn't the phone's fault. She was determined though.

Hanging up again at the lack of answer, she growled at the black screen. This was annoying. Then she thought about it. Where exactly would he keep a phone in a dragon form. Maybe he wasn't back to the ship, or wherever he was going? She'd just crushed his soul. God, that kiss, though. Her fingers rested on her lips as they tingled.

How had she let him leave after that?

Aisha needed to talk to him. She needed to let him know she was just confused, mostly. She also needed him to tell her she could sell this chip. Or maybe she needed to know what the expectations were.

He mentioned labs back home, so she figured out he would

want her to go with him. Fine. But how long would they still be here? And if they went back, and she solved world peace, or at least something, could she bring it back?

She needed to focus. Only she couldn't. Deo wouldn't get out of her head.

"Aisha?"

She jumped as a hand caught her shoulder. "Tan. Don't sneak up on people like that."

He nodded.

"Okay. Sorry. That wasn't my intention, you ran out so fast," he said, keeping pace with her.

"Oh. Yeah. Sorry. Hey, you know what, maybe we should talk? How about tomorrow?"

He nodded. "Why not now?"

She checked her phone again. Nothing still.

"Because, Tan, I have to fix something. But I promise tomorrow."

They walked up to the front lawn and there on her front porch was Deo, nearly naked for the world to see.

*D*eo leaned against the support of her porch. His arms crossed over his chest. He didn't know where she was, but he would wait for her return.

Cy had informed him mid-flight that the phone device they kept for human reasons was ringing with Aisha's number. He hated that device, but it served a purpose. Still, he wasn't about to call her on it when he could drop back in.

This was unexpected. He'd circled back around several times, trying to remove the painful ache in his chest. His dragon fought Deo to go back and claim her. How she had changed her mind this quickly, he would never understand.

Or perhaps she hadn't. He growled at the sight of the small male walking in stride with her. Had she wanted to talk simply to break his heart all over again? Females on this planet were cruel.

He turned away, trying to control himself. The small male was near her again, he'd thought they had a truce. Deo also was fighting the urge to reach out and murder the male. That would not please his mate. Probably.

He sniffed the air. Fear reached him first, and then sadness. The male's scent reached him next, he was the one who smelled of fear whereas Aisha seemed to only have a subtle scent of sadness.Odd. What was she sad about? She'd stomped on Deo's heart, not the other way around.

"Deo?"

He took a deep breath before turning back around. Control. He was a warrior, for shit's sake. He should be the definition of calm. Except when his mate was involved.

"Yes, mate. My brother said you called. I came to answer."

She smiled at him before scowling at Tan.

"Tan. Now isn't a good time."

She rolled her eyes at him. Not a good sign in Deo's experience.

"When is it going to be a good time? We need to talk before you do something you might regret."

She stopped and Deo listened with his dragon's hearing.

"Look, Tan, don't you think that we would both regret getting married just to make my father happy?"

The male scratched his head. "Yeah. No. I agree. I want to be supportive of you, but I don't think we have what we should for a marriage."

Aisha's scent changed, mixing into something new. Something he really didn't understand. His heart on the other hand was very happy to hear Tan finally getting the hint that Aisha would never be his.

"You do?" she asked.

The male nodded.

"I do. Don't get me wrong. I think you're wonderful and you're very smart, but perhaps that thing was right," Tan said.

Deo growled at his comment. How dare something so small call him a thing?

"Tan, he has a name."

Deo watched carefully. He wanted his Aisha to come to him. Leave that feeble male alone. How long was this going to take?

"Well, whatever. Perhaps he was right. I mean, do you think he was right?" asked Tan.

Deo smiled.

"Well, yeah. I agree. But why do you agree suddenly?" she said.

Deo waited for his response.

Tan scratched his head and shrugged. "I guess it's that girl he found." Tan gave Deo a dirty look, but Deo knew the truth. The male simply didn't like that Deo had been right.

But, of course, he'd been right. Aisha's body language had been a female on a mission only moments ago, but now her hands were on her hips and her eyes were narrowed.

He liked the things the male was saying, but he didn't like the distress she was in. Perhaps distress was wrong. Frustrated?

Aisha looked over at him as they got closer, right as Tan's hand reached for Aisha. Deo's feet hit the ground as he ran to stop Tan.

"You will remove your hand from her," Deo said, gripping Tan's wrist.

"Hey. I'm on your side, Deo. Calm down. I just want her to look at me and have her tell me you are what she wants."

Deo clung to the towel around his hips, the only things he could find presentable. With his other hand, he released the male and stood behind Aisha.

She looked over her shoulder at Deo. He didn't want to let her out of his sight, he refused to let the fear that someone could come snatch her from him become a reality.

Truly it was that no matter what, this could all be taken away in a second. She'd already proven that. One moment he thought his world was complete and the next second he was flying back to his ship, alone. What did he do? He clung to this moment as if it was that last bit of hope given to him by the goddess herself.

His hand slipped around her waist, running over her belly.

She leaned into him and his heart fluttered. Could she have truly changed her mind?

Feathering his hand a little lower, his dragon snarled to claim her before she could get away again. Yeah, no. They'd already had this argument.

Deo tasted blood before he realized he bit his own lip trying to fight everything within him. Goddess, he needed her.

"Yes, Tan. He is what I want."

Tan backed away, hands up in surrender. "I'm good with this. I promised your father your happiness. That you wouldn't be alone, and I don't feel that I would do right by him or you if I ignored your wishes."

Aisha's hand wrapped around his forearm, keeping Tan from going.

"What about you though?" she asked.

Tan answered with a smile. "I'll be fine. As much as I want to hate him, whatever he is, he has good instincts. Perhaps I won't be single myself for long."

Deo couldn't see her face, but he could sense the natural perfume of her rather than a storm of emotion. Perhaps she was finally settled with her choices.

Deo's hand splayed against her lower belly. She would not be settling. He was meant for her, and she was meant for him.

His nostrils flared as the scent of the air changed with the breeze. She was not settling. Her body knew he was hers, even if she didn't want to admit it. Her sweet arousal, a light scent on the air, had him drinking it in. He would do anything to love her. His dragon pawed within.

Mine.

Yes. His. He couldn't fight it much longer. Even touching her wasn't keeping the madness down.

He pressed his pelvis against her backside, ensuring she understood his next intention. The second they got rid of this Tan.

"Male? You'll excuse me. Aisha and I have things to discuss."

Tan nodded and held out a hand. Deo studied it, eyeing him. Reaching out he took the offered exchange. This is what humans did in parting and greeting. So he did as expected.

"Treat her well and I won't have any reason to come after you," Tan said, backing away toward the side of the house.

Deo glared. Come after him? He would dare that tiny male to do any of the sort.

Aisha turned in his arms and held a hand to the side of his face.

"Calm yourself. You don't need to growl at him, he's already given you what you want."

Deo couldn't stop the growl. As if Aisha had been his to give.

Deo wouldn't argue with that faulty statement. Not right now. Not with her smelling of sex. Not with a fire burning within his own belly to claim her.

She obviously wanted him back here, and he was done waiting. Deo claimed her lips and lifted her with one quick motion, heading into the house. The door slammed shut as he kicked it, and he moved with determination to her room.

Placing her on her own two feet, he assessed her clothing. His eyes followed his fingers as he flicked each of her buttons open one by one.

One by one he flicked them open, her eyes never leaving his fingers. Sliding his hands under the cotton, he encircled her ribs, running his hands over her skin. Pulling her closer, he pressed his body against Aisha's as he kissed her again.

Running his hand over her back, he reached behind her and yanked at the clasps of the thin lace fabric keeping her beautiful breasts from him. Finally, he was rewarded.

"Yes," she whispered.

The palms of his hands grazed the soft skin as he pulled the lacy fabric up and released her full breasts. He pushed forward, slowly, forcing her backwards to the bed. Laying her back, his lips made a new trail along her neck.

He tasted her skin, inch by inch. As his lips neared her beautiful chest, he licked a trail to a taught peak and nibbled at the sensitive nub. She arched into him, her hands tangling in his hair as she pulled him forward.

Moving lower, he kissed her inch by inch as she wriggled under his touch. Reaching her pants he flicked the button and placed both hands on either side pulling the zipper down. Her scent stronger the lower he went.

A growl rumbled within him. *His.*

Yes, she was his.

Pulling down her pants and panties, he stood up as he slid them off each leg. Licking his lips, his eyes zeroed in the apex of her thighs. He wanted to taste her, all of her.

Kneeling down, he ran his tongue over her slit as he held her hips firm under his grip.

She squirmed as he licked his way around her nub, stroking her lightly at first.

Her hips began to move, pushing against his hand as he circled her entrance with a finger, sliding the digit in and out. She moaned in response and his own dick twitched, begging to be freed.

Looking up from between her legs, he pumped a finger within her faster, his thumb stroking her clit, and her nipples tightening with each stroke. Pushing a second finger in, she bucked against him as he massaged her, adding pressure as he found the rhythm she needed. Her muscles began to tighten around his fingers. A moment later she cried out as her muscles began to pulse and her body quivered.

"Deo," she called out.

Licking his lips, the flavor of her coating his mouth, he reached for the towel around his waist, dropping it to the floor.

Her eyes sparkled as she watched him. Her chest still rose and fell in an uneven, rapid, hasty rhythm thanks to him. Yes, he would ensure his mate was pleased and all her doubts removed one pleasure at a time.

Deo leaned over her, spreading her legs as he settled between them, resting his dick against her stomach. Waiting for her to calm.

He leaned in and whispered into her ear. "Mine."

This time he hoped she understood what he was saying.

"Yes, Deo. I'm yours."

He looked her in the eyes, pulling on all his reserves. If he started, he wouldn't stop. Not this time. He couldn't.

"Do you understand what I offer you, Aisha?"

She nodded. "Yes. No. I don't care as long as it's with you."

He grunted. "You can't go back on this. Once you are mine, you are mine forever."

She nodded. "Yes. Take me. I never want to feel the pain I felt when you left me. My soul ached for you. I never stood a chance."

Placing a kiss on her beautiful mouth, he positioned the head of his dick at her entrance. Running the skin over her opening, letting her wetness run over him as he slowly pushed against her muscles. He moaned in pleasure as her breathing hitched as he pulled out and slid back in.

Aisha's breathing grew ragged even as he took her slowly. The muscles of his arms cording in restraint until he was fully seated.

"More," she said.

If she wanted more, it was more he'd give her. Thrusting in harder this time, she bit down on her lip. Gripping her hands, he held them over her head with one hand as he began a much faster, rougher pace. One where she took every inch of him. He swallowed his own moans of pleasure. Goddess, she felt good.

Aisha tried to pull her hands free, but he wasn't ready yet. She wanted more, and he wasn't done.

As her breath came out shuddering, her muscles tightening around him as he slammed into her one more time, pulling her release from her. Right as he felt her body begin to quiver around him, he slammed in a few more times and right as he was about to release, he lowered his mouth to her shoulder and bit down as he spilled into her.

Mine.

*a*isha allowed Deo to roll them over, mostly because she wasn't able to move. She wasn't even sure she was really here. Nothing on Earth could have ever felt that good. Or could it? Her body was ablaze with senses. Everything around her took on a new feel, look, smell, sound. Her sheets were suddenly coarser than she remembered. His touch warmer than before.

Maybe it didn't matter what happened in her life as long as she had him. Or at least as long as he kept screwing her senseless.

Her mind felt cloudy, like something new was there, but she didn't know what. The itch of magic, stronger than anything she'd ever felt danced along her nerves, refusing to let her ignore it.

Odd.

Slowly, she caught her breath as the muscles between her legs calmed. He was still buried within her. He filled her body so full she still didn't know how he fit. She didn't care. She'd never felt this kind of pleasure, ever.

It only seemed fair, she supposed since the worst pain she'd known was when he'd left that the greatest pleasure she'd ever know was being with him. Losing her own father hadn't felt like her soul had just been ripped away, although it had been painful and devastating, she'd somehow managed to move on and find ways to distract herself.

It had hurt, and she'd been broken, but now, lying here, she realized Deo healed her. Her father was never to be forgotten, but she could live her life again.

Titling her face up, she smiled at Deo.

"How do you feel, mate?" he asked.

She shivered at the way he said mate.

"I dunno. Happy?"

He kissed her forehead.

"Happy is a good thing."

Wiggling against him, she enjoyed the reaction.

"Are you ready already, mate?" he asked.

Oh crap, was she? She just enjoyed seeing him close his eyes in pleasure. Her body was still humming with her own release.

"Are you?" she asked, realizing there was no way he was.

He pushed his pelvis up, and she squeaked.

"I answer the call of my mate's needs. I will always be ready for you."

He rolled over, positioning her on top.

Aisha let a groan of pleasure out as he rubbed against deliciously tender muscles between her legs.

She sat up, pushing him in further, deeper, and her breath caught as she nearly came from the pressure of him within her.

She smirked. "Is this what you had in mind?"

He lifted his hips and pushed into her. She fell forward, her breasts rubbing against the bare skin of his chest. Every nerve within her was alive as she pushed back against him. She wanted more. How could she want more? Closing her eyes, she felt, forgetting where she was, only knowing who was with her.

Her body seemed to know exactly what it wanted from him and needed whatever he gave her.

The palm of his large hands gripped her hips, low, his thumbs resting against her pelvis as he helped push her. He was bringing her to the edge as she sat straight up on him again. Her hips rocking in a rhythm that was exactly what she wanted.

Her body felt sexy as his eyes roamed over her, pushing her to want more. She rested her palm against his pecs as the pleasure built in her, the heat bloomed from between her legs, spreading to her belly until without warning it broke within her and she cried out his name.

He sat up, pulling her against him, lifting her ass and slamming her back down on him.

Oh, God. Too much. It was so much. Could she come for him again? God, it felt so good.

"Yes, Yes." She chanted as her body begged to be used to bring him his own pleasure.

The heat within her burst one more time as he pulled her down in one quick, determined motion as he spilled into her again. This time, though, he leaned back and pulled her with him, closing his eyes.

She echoed him, closing her eyes as she fell into an abyss, listening to the beat of his heart and feeling the heat of him within her.

Her eyes fluttered open, and she realized Deo still snuggled her close. Had they slept? The sun was still up, but lower in the sky. She was almost afraid to move, to wake the beast of a man. Her body still vibrated with pleasure.

Planting a light kiss on his chest, she allowed him to continue to hold her. Aisha hadn't dreamed since her father had passed. As obsession with her work had taken over, her mind had forgotten the art of dreaming. It had forgotten the need for enjoyment.

Realization that she'd been dreaming came as a shock as she continued to wake. Aisha remembered seeing dragons of so many colors, some similar, some different, circling overhead in a sky redder than her own blue Earth sky.

Recognition filtered in like light through gauzy curtains. These weren't her dreams, they were memories. Was this what Deo meant? That once mated, he'd have nothing to hide? Or was it he couldn't hide anything?

Aisha remembered seeing Maddie go quiet, only to have something to say to her mate moments later. Was this connection more than just memories?

The feeling she'd had, the unknown presence, had a name. He was in her head, her Deo. Her mate.

A smirk found its way to her lips. She wouldn't be a scientist if she didn't do any tests. Thinking of something sure to get a reaction, she envisioned herself licking his shaft like a popsicle, taking him in her mouth.

He didn't react, and well, damn it. Now she was horny again and really confused on what this connection thing did.

"Deo?"

"Yes?" he answered.

"Can you read my thoughts?" she asked.

He held her tightly. "No, not yet. But our minds will become linked. You will be able to talk to me here."

Gently, he touched her temple, and then went back to holding her.

"Okay. So. You will know everything I think?"

This was unnerving. Or was it? She wanted to know how to trust him. How could she deny trusting someone she knew everything about?

He rubbed his eyes for a moment. "No. Well, yes. I suppose you can keep some things from your mate, but it takes practice and I see no reason to do so."

She nodded, her cheek against his warm, hard chest.

"Okay. So, right now you can't tell what I am thinking?" she asked one more time.

He shook his head, planting a kiss on the top of hers. "I can feel your feelings, but the bond is still too new."

Her stomach growled. "Are you hungry?" She couldn't remember the last time she'd actually eaten. Her girlish figure would not keep itself up. She laughed to herself at that ridiculous thought. She also felt her face flush as she reveled in the fact that even though she wasn't the skinniest Deo found her sexy and that made her love her body.

Lifting her leg over him, she climbed off of him. He grabbed at her. "I did not tell you to leave, mate," he said, with a teasing tone.

She slapped at his hand. "No. I need some food. Aren't you hungry?"

"Would this make you happy? If I ate?"

She nodded.

"Then I am as well. Shall I help you get food?"

Aisha felt her face heat as she moved off of him. Her legs a bit wobbly.

"No. I'd like to go get it and bring it back to you. Maybe you could put some pants on while I'm gone?"

He smirked. "And why would I do that?"

Shrugging, she took her own advice and grabbed a t-shirt out of a draw. "Because if you stay like that, I don't think we are getting much eating done."

Deo looked around the room. "I can put that odd small blanket on. I did not bring pants when I brought you home in your haste to leave."

Blowing out a breath, she cocked her head. "Fine. Towel it is. Not that it's going to hide much."

She squealed as he reached for her again.

"Nope." And she ran for the door. A manly chuckle, the only thing she heard as she finally got to the hall.

As she walked down the stairs to the kitchen, her previous worries and needs surfaced. She needed to bring up the chip thing, or rather the future of her work. Maybe it wasn't her sole drive anymore, but what if she could still give back to humanity?

Someday?

A lightness in her chest gave way to new clarity. She did need to clear up a few things before she packed up her house, because that almost seemed inevitable.

The creepy guy from her office filtered past her contentment. She really needed to talk to Deo about him. Was that chip his? Did Deo really steal it from a creepy guy who gave off some dangerous vibes?

Aisha hit the last step and suddenly felt woozy. That was strange. Gripping the banister, she held herself up.

A booming voice from her room called out. "Aisha?"

Her lips moved as she meant to say something, but they seemed numb as her legs crumpled under her.

"Aisha?" called the voice. Deo. It was Deo.

His shadow eclipsed the sun streaming into the hall from her door. She needed to answer. Something was wrong, and she didn't know what.

Was she having a heart attack? That would be just fitting. Find your soulmate and then die. No, that wasn't it though.

Another shadow loomed over her and all she heard was a growl coming from above her. Her head swam, the sounds filtering in but as if they were miles away rather than in the same room as her.

Leaning her head against the banister, Aisha struggled to keep it up. A shadow on the floor stretched out as a figure came closer from behind. It was too tall and skeletal to be Deo and should have made her squirm, move away, only her limbs wouldn't respond. After a lot of effort, she could get her head to loll back to see what was happening, until it became too heavy and fell back.

The figure stepped back as something large flew by her. A growl that should have been deafening echoed through the house, but she was too tired. Her head too heavy to see what or who it was.

"Dragon shifter, you are much stronger than we thought. Always stronger. But this time I didn't underestimate you."

She couldn't close her eyes, if she did, she knew that it would all be over and not in a good way. Rolling her head against the wood, she finally saw him. The shadowy figure. It was the creepy man from earlier.

Her eyes began to blur, and she blinked several times. The shadow guy moved further and further away until he was hard to make out. A larger blur, one that she was sure was Deo before he came into focus, stopped next to her. She wanted to cheer him on, only either he was going slower and slower or the world was moving in slow motion.

"I suggest you give into the sleep demons before they overtake your girlfriend here. Would be a pity to waste such a brilliant mind."

Aisha listened again as her body slumped further to the floor.

"No," growled Deo as she watched his form strain. A knee hitting the floor.

"Yes, perhaps she will be of use later. It is a pity she seems to be attached to you, alien."

That voice was creepy man's and it sent chills up her spine, even weak and nearly out of it.

Aisha tried to raise her lead weight of an arm and scratch at him, or at least point a very strategic finger to tell him to fuck off. Neither happened, though.

"Yes. Too bad. Perhaps she will see reason, though. Dragon shifter, we've offered her a very handsome sum for you."

This voice wasn't one she knew though, and it had the power to make her want to run. She wouldn't have, even if she could though. Not while Deo was in danger.

Deo might have said something, she wasn't sure. A static grew around her. Her eyes were so heavy.

She wanted to tell Deo to run, to get away from them. She wanted to tell him that they had offered her money for him, but she'd never have sold him out. But the conversation was in her head. She tried to think it, praying he could hear her already. There was nothing, though. Just more static.

This was fitting. Every time she was happy, fate crapped on her.

She couldn't let the creepy man win. Aisha tried one last time to grip the railing, pulling on any last bit of strength she could muster.

Her hands slid down, her butt hitting the floor. She was useless.

Trying something new, she put her effort into her mouth; she tried to talk again and wasn't sure what words actually came out.

Damn it. She knew that guy had been bad news. Deo was strong though, he should be able to get past this, right?

That had to be the case.

Aisha felt her body going limp as she yawned. No more fight left.

Maybe a five-minute nap would be okay, her brain said. But her heart squeezed in panic. No, no nap. Something was wrong. Deo. He should already be ripping someone to shreds in that dragon form of his. She didn't even care if he destroyed her house.

But sleep sounded so good.

The sharp edge of the stair didn't even feel that uncomfortable right now. Maybe one more minute and then she'd see Deo saving the day.

14

The words ricocheted around his skull.

We offered her a lot of money for you.

He offered his soul to her, and she'd traded him for money? How was that possible? What would this do for her?

Although his mind was trying to fight the sleep demon's powers, his body was losing the battle. Demonic magic wasn't something he knew how to fight well. This wasn't his area of expertise, fighting a non-corporeal being.

He fell to one knee.

Looking back, he watched Aisha struggling until she wasn't. Her hands had grasped to pull herself up, but when that failed she laid her head down and stopped moving.

Was she losing to the magic? Was she giving up? He tried to reach out to her in his mind, but it was blank. Their link still wasn't strong. Or maybe she was sleeping or both.

Fighting against the magic, he started to lose. His other knee hitting the floor. He knew some demons, knew enough to recognize their magic. But his dragon couldn't fight this many of them. His dragon sight could make out their dark shapes, but little else. Anger brewed within him.

"She wouldn't trade me for money," Deo said, his body beginning to shake as it struggled to remain alert.

The man laughed.

"Oh, but she did. Everyone has a price."

He snarled at the man. "How did you find me?"

The man snapped his fingers, and two others came up on either side of Deo.

Deo tried to call his dragon for protection, his scales nearly impenetrable. The dragon tried to answer, but he wasn't able to fully surface, not in this sleepy state.

Deo winced as a stinging sensation poked him in the neck. Fuck. This was going sideways. His neck burned as something worked its way into his system,

Deo called out to his brothers, sending an SOS.

As the first of five voices filtered in, he felt his eyes growing heavy. The last words he heard were enough to shake him to his core.

"Dragon, she led us straight to you," said the man.

Deo couldn't believe it. He wouldn't. But then again, she'd called him back.

But she'd offered herself to him. She'd accepted his mark. No female would be able to break the bond, it would be like cutting off your own arm. No, worse. Sacrificing your own heart.

He tried to answer the call of his brothers, but logic failed.

Trouble. Was all he got out before he accepted this darkness. What good would it do him to fight if the female he loved had given up on him, anyway.

Deo opened his eyes, blinking against the odd lighting. His eyes searched the room. Dirt floor sifted under his claws. He took in the taloned tips of his toes. When had he shifted?

A whimper behind him had Deo shuffling around. A chain

jangled as the woman scrambled back. His heart leapt in anticipation. Aisha, she was with him. She hadn't deceived him.

Only, it wasn't Aisha.

He could feel Aisha, but he needed to block her out. Everything screamed at him to stop. To not ignore his mate. But he couldn't. She would only bring out his weakness.

He lay down as his soul shattered. Laying there with his head resting on his feet, everything came back to him. The struggle. Or the lack thereof. They had finally bested one of them, one of the dragons. Finally figured out a way to beat them. It wasn't the sleep demon magic; it was betrayal. His mate's betrayal.

Emptiness filled him. He had no purpose anymore. He would be a broken warrior if he returned. It would be better to just stay here, keep the Illuminati assholes happy, because without a doubt this was them. Again. Deo had assumed they'd all been destroyed. Warriors knew to never underestimate the enemy, and yet he had.

Although, judging from the current surroundings of metal walls, dirt floor, open ductwork this wasn't below ground nor was it the same type of lab they'd once had.

Deo hadn't seen their first facility, but Kal hadn't been able to block out all his memories of the place. This was very different from Kal's memories.

The female sniffled again. Deo lifted his head and sniffed. The dragon snorted out the wretched scent of fear.

What was she afraid of?

He rested his giant dragon head on his front legs again, waiting. They weren't after her. Perhaps she was a snack?

It took him a few moments to sift through his still sleepy system. They weren't stupid, and it was doubtful they thought he ate humans, so what did they want with a human and why was she in here?

His dragon sighed as he shifted into human form, the argument from his beast that they were more susceptible in their two-legged human form. Deo agreed, but he needed answers.

As he moved closer, the woman skittered back into the corner, not that she could get away as chains jingled with her every movement.

"Who are you?" he asked. He kept his voice quiet and gentle hoping it would help.

She whimpered.

His lips formed a straight line as he thought.

"Look. I'm not here to hurt you. I will however do my best to save you, if you tell me who you are?"

Her teeth chattered.

Running his hand down his face he fought to control his frustration. He'd lost his mate today. He'd lost his freedom. What else would he have to lose that mattered?

He stepped closer, and the girl cowered. Damn it. This wasn't going well, like everything else.

Deo felt the tug from his brothers' mental connections. He closed them off. Right now, he couldn't deal with them. Didn't want them to find him. Not until he had any idea where here was or what they wanted from him. He would protect them.

There was no tug however from his mate. Nothing. He sucked in the air against the tightness in his throat, trying to ignore the stabbing in his chest. He braced himself against the nearest cold metal wall as he tried to push it all away.

Push away the fact that his whole world had made sense for a few hours until it no longer did.

Deo did not do weak. He couldn't afford to on the battlefield, he couldn't do it now. Not when he knew that this wasn't good. Whatever it was. It wasn't good.

"Female, I will not hurt you. Give me a moment to free you."

He bent down, focusing on the issue in front of him. He wouldn't allow this female to suffer at the hands of whatever evil lurked around this place.

Following the chain with his eyes, he traced the metal encircling a large pipe. She couldn't move away any further, so that part was less complicated.

He held a hand out as if calming a small animal. She didn't move, her saucer-like eyes following his every move.

Picking up the chain he pulled, two metal links breaking apart.

She gasped in surprise.

"I promise you, I am not the one to fear here."

She nodded and appeared to have finally stopped quivering like a slight wisp of a tree caught in a windstorm.

"Thank you," she whispered.

He nodded and flopped down.

"What do you know of this place?" he asked.

She nodded up to the ceiling, his own eyes following as he traced the room. A camera. Seemed fitting.

"You're a dragon?" she asked.

Deo turned his attention back to her. She needed to be calmer if he was going to get her out alive, so perhaps a simple chat may give him some time to assess the situation further.

"Yes. And you?" Deo sniffed the air. "Are human?"

She nodded.

"Are you with them?" he asked.

She shook her head.

Keeping his voice low, he whispered. "Have you seen them?"

She gave a nod as she pulled her knees tighter into her chest. "There are only two that I have seen. Also, screaming hasn't gotten any attention, so I assume we are somewhere in an empty warehouse."

"Why are you here?" he asked.

She shrugged. "I don't know. One minute I was walking home from school, I'm a teacher, and the next thing I know I'm here."

"But you are human? Why would this group want you?" Deo wondered what they were up to. This wasn't the same pattern as before. He knew it was tied together, though. They made it clear that they didn't know him, but they knew of the brothers. They'd mentioned how they did not or would not underestimate their powers. He was still certain they were in the same group as before.

Deo had to hand it to them. They didn't give up easily.

The female continued. "I didn't even see them coming. One minute I was grabbing my keys and the next minute I woke up here," she said, wiping her eyes. She wasn't crying. But she obviously had.

"Well, give me a few minutes to figure out what we are up against. I promise you, I will get you out alive."

She scratched at the crook of her arm.

"What's that? Are you okay?" He pointed to the space she itched.

Looking down, her fingers ran over a red spot where small odd colored lines had spread from.

"I don't know. I woke up with it. Maybe it's a spider bite?"

He nodded, but it didn't look like a spider bite. Not even a little. It looked like more black magic. Darkness. He sniffed the air again, finding foreign scents that he'd never encountered.

Listening, though there was little to hear. No whispers. No air vents flowing. Creaks of an old building. Wind blowing through a crack or hole. He couldn't make out any traffic. Not near anything it would appear. This was complicated if he couldn't figure out how she would get to safety even if he could get her out of the room to begin with.

"We will wait for a bit, see what they want. I will not hurt you, but until I know what we are up against, I will not set you free without any chance of rescue. Is anyone looking for you?"

Another shake of her head. "No. I mean, there's a chance that my school will start looking if I don't report back by Monday. But, no. No one else will look for me."

He closed his eyes and pinched the bridge of his nose. Walking to the camera, he looked up and growled.

"What do you want from us?"

Nothing, but then he didn't exactly expect much. Hell, this wasn't like before, so he expected nothing like it.

A few minutes passed. He tested the walls again. They weren't thin, but they weren't that thick either. What if he punched right through it? Got her to safety and then returned to keep them from chasing his family.

"I wouldn't do that, dragon," came a familiar voice. The same voice from Aisha's house as he was thrust into an oblivion. He whipped around and didn't see anyone, but then he saw the large hold on the door. How had he missed that?

Five strides and he stood front and center of the door. Would he be able to reach his arm through there and rip the guy's throat out? Possibly.

"Dragon, I highly suggest you choose not to act on whatever is going through that thick skull of yours. We have a proposition for you."

A rumble rolled up his throat. "A proposition?"

The man smirked, or perhaps that was his smile. Deo sniffed the air and retched at the scent of dark magic and decay. The man spoke, distracting Deo for a moment.

"Yes. All you need to do is mate with that female. You give us what we want, and you are free to leave."

Anger burned away his revulsion to make way for pure rage. His dragon screamed. His arms scaled up and Deo held the dragon in the limbo between their human and dragon forms.

"And, if I don't?" he asked.

The man's smile fell. "Then you are signing not only your death warrant but hers as well."

Deo looked back at her, scared, cowering, innocent.

"Why her?" Deo asked.

The man shrugged. "Wrong place at the right time. We would

have used one of our own, but your little hoard of dragons has all but wiped out our numbers."

That gave Deo a burst of pride, but also understanding. "Why can't you leave my brothers and me alone?"

A man that Deo swore he recognized from Kal's memories pushed into view of the small peek-through door.

"Why? Why? Because you are what I've searched for far too long. A superior species. I intend to create the perfect being, and your species is an integral part."

He rolled his neck as a chill ran down his spine. "Perhaps you should let this go. I will not mate with the female."

The man's face twisted, his eyes growing cold.

"The scientist traded you for money. Why do you remain loyal to someone who doesn't want you?"

Closing the slight gap between himself and the door, Deo braced his hands on the door frame and peered through. "You underestimate my species. We are devoted to our mates and to the freedoms of others. Regardless if I am wanted or not, I will never harm another."

The familiar male's pasty skin appeared to color with a tinge of pink. He was alive. Information Deo would continue to catalogue against this enemy.

"Look dragon, all I ask is for a small favor. Give me what you have taken from me, and I will let you walk out of here."

Deo snarled. "I have taken nothing from you and what's stopping me from walking out of here, anyway?"

The man, Dr. Rollings if he recalled correctly from Kal, did not appreciate his defiance.

"I have control over several demons. If you try, I will release them. Perhaps you are not as affected by them, but she wouldn't survive. Are you really a superior species if you sacrifice someone for your own freedom?"

Deo stood still, thinking. Could he do this? Risk her for his own life. He wasn't even trying to escape. He could not. He would not take another, though. He only wanted his Aisha, but he couldn't let this female die because of him.

He didn't want this woman to suffer. An innocent never deserved to suffer.

"I would not sacrifice her for my own freedom, but I will also not give you what you want," Deo said.

The doctor's ashen skin shifted for a second, a blink of an eye and it was gone. It had turned to something even more repulsive, gone so fast Deo wasn't sure what he'd even seen.

"There is no demonic magic in this room?" Deo asked, unsure he'd get an answer. Perhaps pushing an evil scientist too much was never an excellent idea. Deo wasn't sure how the man was alive after their last attack. Perhaps that was why he was so pale? Trying to remember him the way Kal did though, everything was tainted. Blurred with the rage of Kal's dragon's memories.

"I think we are done for now. Just remember, if you choose not to do as asked, she won't survive and I can't guarantee you will either," said the doctor as he reached for the sliding closure to the hole.

Deo looked back at her. She didn't exactly look healthy as it was.

"What have you done to her?" he asked, as if he could help without any medical equipment.

Dr. Rollings stepped forward. "I don't have to answer to you, dragon. But if you must know, it's a little concoction of my own. You've seen a variation of it in my other daughters, although one is much more successful than the other."

Deo knew he meant Lilly, and his stomach churned again. This man was much worse than they'd given him credit. A far larger threat than originally thought.

Against his better judgement, Deo realized he couldn't conceal this from his brothers. He couldn't allow them to be subject to another surprise and it looked like surrender wasn't going to be an option for him either.

Deo backed away from the door, the whites of the doctor's eyes the only thing he could see through the square hole.

Walking back to the girl, she flinched.

"I don't want to die," she said, her words feeble.

He nodded. "That is not in the plan."

She smiled and stood up. Brushing herself off.

"I want to say I am a big enough person to just let you do what they ask and then leave so at least one of us gets out. But would you come back for me?"

He shuddered. Yeah. She was cute. Yes, the thought might have crossed his mind as one of a million options that wouldn't work. He wouldn't touch her, he couldn't. His heart was claimed, even if she didn't want him anymore.

"That also isn't an option. Just hold tight."

15

Her stomach wretched as she tried to stand up. Nothing came out. It couldn't. She was down to stomach acid and vital organs. None of which would settle her.

Pulling herself up the banister, her legs wobbled. What had just happened? Her hands white-knuckled the wood as she fought to keep herself up. This felt like carbon monoxide poisoning. She'd had that once long, long ago. To this day, she couldn't forget it. Only thing was, none of her detectors had gone off.

Looking around, her eyes tried to focus on what was missing. Something was missing. Her lungs burned as she sucked in air. Deo. Deo was missing.

The flood of nightmares, or rather questionably lucid memories broke free of a mental dam creating a deluge of everything that had happened.

She jumped as electric shock pricked against her skin, up and down her arms, along every nerve. She screamed out in pain.

The edges of her vision clouded as she tried to focus on the hall.

Slowly, though, the pain subsided to a memory.

Holding up her hand, she studied it. Nothing seemed different, but as she studied her own skin, she saw it. Her skin had a faded halo around it.

She wiped at her cheek as she realized a tear had escaped. No. She didn't cry.

She was fine.

But what was going on? Her magic flared along her fingers.

Swallowing, she thought back, relying on the little knowledge she had about being a witch. She didn't know anything complex, most of her training had been independent and revolved around healing magics.

Her throat burned as she swallowed again, realizing a desperate need for water. This felt like a damn hangover now. What had happened?

She'd seen the creepy guy, seen a few other shadowy men, but what was the magic that could bring Deo to his knees?

Memory spells. She knew something like that. Mumbling a few words, she watched as the surrounding air shifted and restructured into muted visions of what had happened.

The creepy guy from the lab. His mouth moved but sadly the memory had no sound. Well, shit.

She squinted, trying to read his lips.

Remember. Why couldn't she remember this? She'd been there. He was talking to her. Maybe? Turning her head, the vision of Deo charging him in near slow motion choked a sob in her throat. He was trying to save her.

Her hand flew to her chest as she watched him, her huge warrior, her dragon brought to his knees.

It was then that she saw the strange distortions in the vision. What was there? She couldn't make it out. Something didn't feel right.

Standing there, she watched the memory replay again and again. What was it?

Her phone. She could call the other dragons. They would help her.

Stepping back from the banister, she pushed herself up the stairs to where her phone should be. Her breathing grew heavier as she moved the lead weights of her feet up one step at a time.

Pausing on the top step, she stopped and caught her breath. Her magic was still sparking around her, warning her? No. Maybe? She didn't know. It wasn't like her being a half human-half witch hybrid ever got her accepted into any magical schools. Or, well, perhaps it was the fact her dad didn't exactly know what to do either.

Something had drugged her. She needed to heal, later. Deo first. She needed a plan. Grab her phone and then head to the kitchen. She knew how to flush the system against certain magical toxins and the more she listened to her magic the more it made sense. Demonic magic. That's why nothing seemed like it should, there were traces of demonic magic here, in her, around her. It made sense that something not from this world would be able to take down Deo.

Nothing else could have done something like that.

Phone. She needed to get to the phone.

A few more steps and she leaned on her doorjamb. So close. She bit back the stomach acid trying to come up.

No. She wasn't getting sick, again. Not while Deo was missing. That's what the pain was. It wasn't the demonic magic; it wasn't her own magic; it was that he was in trouble.

She didn't know why she knew that. The mark on her shoulder tingled as her magic danced around it.

Of course she knew- she was connected to him. Right. Mated. She needed him. She wanted him back.

Stumbling to the nightstand, she grabbed at her phone and sat on the bed, or more like flopped. The scent of Deo on her sheets caught her off guard and she gasped for air as her throat grew tight. What if he wasn't okay? What if she'd really screwed everything up? But she hadn't. She hadn't accepted that asshole's offer, but she also hadn't been honest with Deo, not right away.

Her eyes blurred as she tried to scroll through her phone to look for the number he'd given to her. She prayed someone answered.

It rang. She focused on the sound, trying to control the panic swallowing her.

More ringing, until, finally. "Hello?"

"Oh, thank God. Deo is missing."

Silence met her. Did he hang up? Whoever answered better not have or she would kill them, later of course. She didn't even care who answered; it had to be one of the dragons.

"Is this Eadric? Hello?"

Finally, his voice answered. "This is Cy. We will come to you." And without another word, he hung up.

Cy? Who was Cy? How many of them were there? Whatever. Didn't matter, she supposed.

Okay. What did she need? Pants. She needed pants. The room suddenly seemed chilled. Was it her? Or was it the absence of her dragon?

Her body shivered.

Taking all of her energy she stumbled to her closet and grabbed whatever was closest. Who cared what she looked like right now.

Stumbling out, she struggled to get one foot in front of the other quickly. The room spun a bit, but she refused to give in.

"Shit," she said as she just barely made it to the bed where she face-planted.

"Aisha? Wake up."

She rolled over, her head splitting.

"Oh, thank goodness. You're alive," said the same female voice.

"Of course she's alive, she was breathing," said another female.

Aisha blinked away the sleep, or haze of whatever had just happened.

"Is that you, Maddie?"

The voice came into focus.

"Yes. Lilly too. The boys are downstairs, waiting."

She rolled her head to one side. "Waiting for what?"

Maddie's wild eye expression came into focus.

"For you. They need you to track Deo."

She shook her head. "I can't feel him."

Aisha didn't need to see the look Maddie was giving her. It was either a big you're stupid look, or one of pity. She didn't want either.

"Yeah. They'll explain. Let Lilly and I help you downstairs."

Slowly, Aisha pushed herself up.

"I really think I screwed up. Why can't I feel him? Shouldn't I be able to feel more than whatever this is?"

Maddie and Lilly looked at each other.

"Let's get you downstairs and maybe they can answer your questions," answered Maddie.

A subtle nod was all she could manage as the two women put an arm around her.

She was okay. Her legs no longer felt weighted down. That was good. The stabbing pain in her chest grew though the more she sobered up, as if whatever the magic that had put her in her drugged state had also suppressed her connection to Deo.

She bit down on her lower lip, holding the pain in.

"Aisha, tell us what you know," asked one of Deo's brothers.

She shook her head. There was no way she could tell them what had happened. Instead, she pulled away from the two women and took a deep breath as she called on her newly found magic, one that flowed through her much stronger than ever before.

Flicking her wrist, the images of earlier replayed. Each of the warriors jumped at first, moving out of the way.

The same image of Deo being brought to his knees played again, and it was almost too much to watch. She'd failed him and he was paying whatever that price might be.

They each watched as the series of events replayed once more, over and over. This was being caught in her own nightmare.

Hugging herself, she sucked in the pain.

Searching within her she tried to use her magic to call out to him. It wasn't like she understood what his mark meant, but she should have something. He'd said as much. She'd watched Lilly and Maddie, there should be something else there. But nothing.

Aisha had never felt this alone, not even when she had been single and her father hundreds of miles away. This was the feeling of true emptiness, like part of you was broken.

"This is the doctor," growled one of the men, Kal, she thought she remembered. As Maddie walked to his side Aisha was certain she was correct.

"How did he survive?" asked another, one that she didn't think she knew. Maybe that was Cy? His voice was familiar.

Lilly came from around Aisha. "I don't know. He's a monster, I don't know that there is an easy answer when it comes to father."

Eadric closed the gap between Lilly and himself, passing Aisha in the process and her shattered heart. He reached out for his mate and held her. Something Aisha desperately needed from Deo. Regret for even considering selling the chip joined the endless parade of pain and sadness.

But, no. This might have still happened. If only she'd destroyed the chip somehow instead of keeping it just in case she figured out that last missing compound. Her drive to not fail, caused her to lose the most important thing. Love.

She'd been so focused on herself. On her work, on her need for Deo, and her need to ensure that she would get what she wanted, that in the end she failed to see all the signs around them. Failed to see a monster in human skin.

She jumped at Eadric's hand on her shoulder. "Aisha, can you tell us where he is?"

She swallowed a sob and called on her reserve of strength.

"No. I don't know. I just have a number to contact that, that thing. Doctor?" She pointed to the magical representation of the guy.

Eadric didn't remove his hand, and although Aisha appreciated the comfort, it was wrong. It wasn't Deo.

"Call out to him, here," he pointed to her temple.

She lifted a brow. "In my head? It's that easy?"

Lilly gave a reassuring half smile.

Closing her eyes, she tried.

Deo? Are you there?

Nothing. She tried again.

Deo? Please. Answer me.

Nothing. She held herself tighter as the churning in her belly worsened.

"What happened before he was taken? He did mate you, did he not? We can feel the bond, his scent is all around you," Eadric said.

Aisha wanted to be offended, but that wouldn't do them any good. "Yes." She pointed to her shoulder.

Eadric lifted a sleeve on her other arm. "Sorry, but I needed to check. His marking is here as well. Your mating has been completed. You should be able to communicate with him-"

"Unless," said another.

She shot a steely look at the guy. "Unless what?"

A man, a dragon with more gray eyes than orange held his hands up, palms out.

"Unless you rejected him?"

Her eyes flew wide. "What? No. I wouldn't. I couldn't. Can a woman even do that after this point?"

The man shrugged. "There are rumors of how a rejection might work, it's just never happened. A fated mate is chosen by the goddess. There should never be a need. But you're pale and you stink of something sour."

This time she snarled. "Well excuse me for not looking my

best after being attacked and losing the love of my life only a few hours after figuring it all out. I didn't reject him. This man, this doctor. He offered me money, loads and loads of it and all for Deo. And I said no. I didn't know he was here. I didn't know he followed me. Or, or maybe it was this stupid fucking chip." She shuffled over to the door where her bag lay on the floor. She yanked at it and pulled the dish out and thrust it at the man accusing her. "It wasn't my fault. It was that guy. I mean, how was Deo not strong enough to beat him?"

Lilly stepped forward. "Aisha, calm down. No one is accusing you. It's okay. We're just trying to understand. But I think I can help at least."

Breathing heavily, Aisha returned her arms around her body, suddenly realizing the cold seeping back in. Emptiness.

"Do you see those figures in the, well, this magical thing?" Lilly asked.

Aisha shook her head in unison with the lot.

"Those are demons. I. Hold on," Lilly said as she stepped over to Aisha. "May I?" She motioned to Aisha's arms, and all Aisha could do was shrug.

Lilly placed both hands on Aisha's forearms and closed her eyes. Aisha's body heated, slowly at first until it reached an uncomfortable level. Sweat beaded on her brow and a scream caught somewhere between her mouth and throat as just as quickly as the heat grew to a blaze, it backed away.

"Sorry," Lilly mouthed.

How much more was she supposed to take as her legs wobbled. Aisha appreciated the firm hands holding her up. Not the right hands was all her brain could think, but at least she was upright.

"Do you feel the magic?" Lilly's voice broke through the haze.

Aisha felt nothing, literally nothing. The cold empty creeping further into her body as she started to shiver.

"I feel it. Do you?" said someone.

"Yes. Demonic traces. Deo would know exactly what this was. Who else knows about this shit?" boomed another.

Lilly's soft voice spoke again. "It's a sleep demon. My father used them on me sometimes. I remember now. He stopped using demons when he figured out I could do things I wasn't supposed to be able to."

Everyone turned to Lilly and stared like they had never heard anything so crazy before.

"Okay. So, we have a demon tamer and dragons. Maddie, what do you do?" Aisha asked.

She flicked her hair over her shoulder. "I, my dear, am a witch, but I think you might know that. You're one too, aren't you?"

Aisha faltered. "I. Well, yes. But I'm not powerful."

Maddie took a few more steps forward. "This kind of magic," said Maddie, pointing to the memory spell. "Is not from a weak witch. I bet you just didn't know. Fate plays tricks on us. Sometimes we can't see who we really are until we've found the one that brings the true us out."

The ache hit Aisha hard, the cold finding the core of her soul and pushing out the remaining fire in her soul. Buckling over, she let out a strangled cry.

Words flew around her, but she couldn't focus on who they came from.

"What's happening to her?"

A male voice said, "She's ice cold."

Another voice said, "Deo's in danger, that we can be sure of."

"Aisha, I need you to focus on the source of the pain. We will need you to help direct the others. He isn't answering anyone."

She nodded as someone grabbed her, helping her out the door. She barely focused on anything other than someone was picking her up.

"Hold on, okay?"

A familiar texture of rough scales met her hands as she sat atop not her blue dragon, but a more purple tinted almost black dragon. Aisha didn't have time to think as she nodded and focused on the pain. What did it mean?

The dragon jerked beneath her and she squeezed her legs tight around him, leaning close to his body. This felt wrong, but there was no other way. She understood that, but it felt wrong.

"Aisha, which way?" yelled Maddie as an orangish dragon came up next to them.

If she wasn't in so much pain, this would be the most beautiful and unbelievable sight.

They circled the sky as Aisha did as asked and felt with her soul. After two full rotations, she finally could feel the difference and pointed into the direction where she could feel what she thought might have been his heartbeat in her soul.

$\mathcal{D}$eo tried to reach out to his brothers. There was nothing. Strange.

What could keep him from them? The human female wasn't looking healthy either. The blackish streaks seemed to grow.

What had they done to her? What had they done to him? There was a sound at the door, and he shifted into his dragon before they came closer.

He backed into the corner, trying to shield the female. Her life mattered regardless of what these assholes thought. He faced the door, ready for a fight.

"I grow tired of waiting, dragon. I also assumed this would be a problem. Nothing you creatures do is easy."

Deo's dragon's head moved side to side, watching the doctor move. He sucked in some air and readied to use his fire.

"I wouldn't do that if I were you dragon. At best you can get me. Although I do appear to not be affected by your fire, or my daughter's, for that matter. Curious, isn't it? And perhaps you miss the female. But at worst you torch her, or me and never find out how to get out of here alive. And I assure you. You will not. Your time is running out, dragon. I will be departing. Should you fulfill my wish, I will fulfill my promise of release? Do not take her though. The demons here, they will attack."

Deo growled and his dragon crouched low. They wanted to rip this male limb from limb.

"Yes. Well, goodbye, dragon. I await a report from my colleague. I have other work to deal with. If I were you, I would push aside these silly notions of true mates and save your-self. After all, I am not asking for you to claim her. Just simply do whatever it is you do to make offspring. You know, children. Like the ones you took from me."

Smoke poured from his dragon's nostrils as he held in the anger.

The skeletal figure of the doctor walked out, leaving Deo to check the choices he had.

His dragon circled the room. Sniffing each corner, looking for a weakness. The nasty scent of decay, what he was realizing may very well be demon scent, had his dragon pawing at his nose. Why they didn't enter the room he wasn't sure, but he was certain it wouldn't last.

Deo walked over to the next wall and stood on hind legs. He sniffed at the ceiling. He tried to reach out to his brothers again. And still nothing. If he had to guess, the demons were the issue. Good thing to note for their future expeditions and battles. Find ways to battle demons.

That wasn't helping right now, though.

The dragon dropped to all fours again, swinging his tail around and hitting the wall. Some dust, a possible crack, but not the hoped-for hole. He turned to a gentle touch on his tail.

"My name's Jenn. Could you turn back into a human?"

His dragon felt like at this point they had done what they could, for the moment anyway. A second later he was in human form.

"I am Deo," he said.

She smiled, her dirt covered face showed streaks of more tears.

"I. Uh, well. I know I'm not what a guy like you would want. But I could maybe help? There's no use in both of us dying here."

Deo cocked his head. What was she talking about?

"You are an exquisite female. A male would be more than lucky to have you as a mate. I have a mate or, well-" he broke off. Closing his eyes, he breathed away the pain in his heart. He had a mate that didn't want him, or at least not enough to trust him to give her what she needed. His entire life was a duty before your own needs until his mate. Suddenly his need for her came above all things, and then his new mission was to serve her. Make her happy and he'd failed. He hadn't succeeded and it not only hurt to fail, but the brokenness inside of him might rip him apart.

"I can't release you until I understand the demons," he finally finished.

She shook her head. Deo watched her as she unbuttoned the now dirt brown shirt.

"I didn't mean for me to get out of here. I told you my name so that someone would remember me. I already tried to get away once and I won't try again. I don't even understand what happened. Something was in my head. I couldn't see straight. The walls came alive and attacked me. I can't do that again," she said.

Deo knew at once what was out there. Fear demons. Well, at least the doctor stuck with what worked. Only thing was, that still made no sense as to why he couldn't communicate with his brothers.

Deo shook his head as something tried to break through.

His eyes grew wider and her fingers shook worse and worse as she got to the last button. She discarded her shirt. "I'm not afraid of you. You seem like a good person, dragon, whatever it is you are. If you do as he asks, you can go free."

Understanding creeped in as she unbuttoned her pants.

"No. Stop!" he shouted.

He took two steps forward and grabbed her hands, holding them within his own.

"No. No woman should ever be used. No woman should ever have her choices taken from her."

She smiled. "Yeah. Well. I am making this choice, though. I mean, I've never been in love. I really don't have anyone to miss me and I love kids. Maybe this is okay?"

A shiver ran up his spine.

"Jenn, no. They will use you and discard you once they are done. This is not someplace you can simply just live."

She looked up into his eyes.

"Whoever your, was it mate? Whoever she is, she's lucky."

Her eyes cast down and Jenn pulled her hands free of him.

Turning her back, her shoulders shook as sob after sob racked her body. The sound of anguish filling the prison like room.

Deo didn't know what to do. Why was she crying?

"Jenn. I am sorry. Did I hurt you? Are you okay?" he asked as he hesitantly reached for her shoulder again.

"No. No, I'm not okay. I'm so ugly that you won't even have me to save your own life. How is a woman supposed to take that? I can't even die here thinking that maybe in another life I might have found someone to love me."

He turned her around, slowly. She didn't fight. He was certain the fight in her had been exhausted.

"It's not that I don't find you beautiful. I meant it. You are very pleasing to the eye. Understand though that once a dragon's heart is claimed, he is bound to his mate heart, mind, and soul. To break that bond would be a fate worse than death."

And it was true. He knew that. So why, even with Aisha's denial, was he still standing? Why was he able to get through the pain? Perhaps he was wrong. Did he dare think that?

She sniffled. "I'm sorry. But would it be worse to never see her again?"

Deo stopped to think about this. Was the anguish within him

now based purely on his own false conclusions? Was it pain he felt or the sorrow perhaps from the effects of the demon magic here? He felt deep within himself, truly searched every corner of his soul and there within the magic he could still sense her.

Something wasn't what it seemed. And at this moment he roiled in conflicted thought. Did he try to escape and know for certain he would seal this female's death? He couldn't be with her, though. Beautiful or not, it wasn't an option.

"Would you say you trust me?" he asked.

She nodded. "You seem okay," she said.

Well, did she really have a choice? She was between a demon and a dragon. Life wasn't getting less complicated for this woman.

"What exactly did you see out there, when you tried to escape?"

Her skin paled.

"I, it was awful. It was like everything that I didn't even know I was afraid of filled my head. Everything was out to get me. I was alone, but people were everywhere. Honestly, I'm not even sure if this place has a way out."

Her arms wrapped around her midsection.

"Put your shirt back on, because we are getting out of here. I'm prepared to handle these demons."

She shook. "I don't think they are the only monsters here though. He mentioned that if I had gotten too far, there were others."

Deo would need to risk it. He would do whatever he had to to find his mate. He would do whatever it took to save this innocent female too. He would not leave her behind.

"We will have to risk it. I can't reach my brothers within this cell and perhaps whatever guards us may not be everywhere. We will need to hope and pray to the goddess."

She trembled but did as he asked. "Goddess?" Jenn asked as she slipped an arm through the shirt sleeve.

"The one who blessed us," he said. Stepping back, he tried to smile reassuringly. "When I shift, climb on my back, stay down, close your eyes, and hold on."

Jenn nodded. Habit had him sniffing the air, and he knew in one quick gulp of air, that she was terrified. Hopefully, it wasn't of his dragon, because that would make this much more difficult.

With that last thought, he shifted. Turning, his dragon patiently waited for her. She approached with caution, and his dragon tried to hide his impatience. As she got closer, he put an arm out to allow her easier access.

His dragon rolled his eyes as if she was the only thing between him and his mate. Which wasn't the case, but Deo couldn't reason with the damn beast some days.

A quick wiggle check to not only see that she was seated, but for something else and Deo wanted to slap the damn creature. Deo knew his dragon was proving a point that she wasn't meant to be there for long. Fucking dragons.

Heading to the door, he eyed it and blew a steady stream of fire against the metal. Jenn whimpered, but he hoped she was smart enough to do as he asked and keep her head down. He didn't have time to worry. She either did as asked, or perhaps she would be nursing a few more injuries. At least she would be alive.

Stopping the steady attack on the metal, the door glowed red as he punched his clawed foot toward it. The thing gave way, warping and opening.

He wouldn't fit through the door in this form, but he didn't care. Pushing through hot metal wasn't a concern as the wall tore to accommodate his massive shoulders.

He snuffed as the acrid scent of demons. It was everywhere. Good thing his dragon was ready. They used their other senses to find the exit. Sounds took on a unique design as he waited to understand what the air's motion did around these creatures. He waited for them to become something other than air and shadow, anything to help him see them versus the area around them.

Deo's dragon moved in the direction of calmer air for now, assuming he would either end up with a better chance to reach his brothers or there was a way out.

Jenn squeezed tighter on his back. It took another moment before he could feel the effects of the demonic magic.

Pushing himself, they moved quickly, trying to push away the nightmares playing at the edge of his mind. He knew what the fear was from. He could reason through it, as long as he focused on his mate and the hope that nothing was as it seemed.

He took a deep breath as they moved between the fear demons and something new. Anger burned through him. He needed something to fight as the labyrinth of tricks was growing frustrating.

His senses told him they weren't alone, but he also didn't know what they were fighting. Looking up, it was clear they were in a basement without hope of a window. Wonderful.

Reaching out for his brothers, there was still nothing.

Jenn squeezed his sides harder, and he pressed on, knowing whatever was in this part of the basement was getting to her far sooner than it got to him.

He moved quickly, stopping as a voice called to him.

"Deo. Come to me, Deo."

No. This was not real. Right?

He turned, following the voice. "Deo. Come to me, Deo."

It was Aisha's voice; he wanted to follow. Was she here? Had she come for him? As they moved closer, his dragon froze. The scent was wrong.

"Deo. Come to me, Deo."

He snarled as something lashed out in a white fog.

He backed away as the sense of danger sunk in.

Jenn screamed somewhere off in the distance. No wait.

Shaking his head thoroughly, he realized it was Jenn on his back.

Looking around, Deo took in the corridor. Shit. They had gotten sucked in.

Something lashed out again, tentacle-like arms reached out of the fog. No.

Not today, demon.

His dragon reared up, turning them around. Jenn slipped, but as he slammed back down, he felt her sink her heels into his sides. They needed to get out of here.

He tried to get back to listening. Using senses other than his eyes. All around them was fog, but if he concentrated hard, the magic thinned to the right of him. He followed.

The building was a mix of demon decay and sour fear from Jenn. He tried to hurry. Finally, as they rounded another corner and through an area of old rusted pipes, he found stairs.

They paused in wait for the trap. It didn't take long for one to manifest. The room moved and shivered around them. The stairwell moved even though they stood still. He could see the shimmer of the black magic as near invisible creatures circled round and round, waiting to strike. It was doubtful that Deo could get through the stairs as his beast, but what of Jenn. She'd fit, but could she do it? Could she get through this hoard of demons? He wasn't sure and didn't want to risk it.

A quick moment passed as he formed his plan. Reaching around in a quick jerk, he pulled her pants by his teeth. She let out a yelp of surprise. The whites of her eyes were red. The apparent suffering within her burdened him more than he wanted.

She stood still as he reached his tongue out and lapped at her. She didn't scream; and he was grateful. He coated her in his saliva, praying this would work for his next plan. After she seemed fully covered and somewhat stunned, he nudged her with his muzzle to ensure she didn't fall over. Petrified might have been a good way to describe her, and at this moment, perhaps helpful.

Seconds were lost as he shifted somewhere between human and dragon. He wasn't getting his hide through the narrow space.

Crouching low, he pulled her near motionless body toward him, placed her belly to his back. Deo didn't have time to wonder if she'd be able to hold on, but when he fastened her arms around his neck, she clasped her hands. She was following on some level, even if she appeared to be missing in action.

As he secured one leg with an arm, he stood and readied himself to sprint. Pulling in a lengthy breath, he let his fire cover the entire space. Next, he chased his fire and prayed to the goddess that Jenn would survive.

Sharp pain stung his sides as things lashed out, scratching him beyond the barrier of his frame. They needed out.

He reached out to his brothers once more as they hit the landing.

Brothers?

Nothing, but then a voice that brought him a sense of hope.

Aisha?

17

The vice around Aisha's ribcage released at the sound of Deo's reply.

Aisha is that you?

Relief washed over her. It was his voice in her head. All the shouting to the wind hadn't been for nothing. Halfway here she'd wondered if she was a helium atom short of an electron, unstable, but finally it all paid off.

Yes, it's me. I can hear you.

The sick feeling in her stomach persisted, and it had little to do with the dips the dragon she rode took.

"Aisha, he's reaching out. They found him," said Maddie.

"I know. I can hear him, he's here." She pointed to her head as she bit back tears. He was alive.

Maddie smiled. "Finally," she said.

Kal took off suddenly as the dragons changed their positions. Aisha watched as they moved, flying two by two.

She burped and covered her mouth trying to keep her stomach where it was as she watched the ground grow closer

Aisha? I need to hear your voice.

Right okay. Whatever he wanted.

You're okay? We're coming. I think we're close, she thought.

There was a silence for a moment and then her head swam. No. She wasn't going to sleep this time. Wait. No. This wasn't her, this was Deo.

Deo, fight it. Fight the feeling. We're almost there.

The feeling cleared.

Yes, close. You are close. I feel you.

She looked around as they hovered over what looked to be an old factory, or rather a small abandoned group of industrial buildings.

Deo. Talk to me? Are you okay?

A soothing calm came over her for a moment. It faded as quickly as it came on her. Instead she shuddered as images, broken and disjointed of teeth surrounded and snapped at her. Razor sharp, monstrous.

Deo, what is that? Is that what you see?

Instead of an answer, she held in a scream as the images blurred. He was running, but running where? She couldn't tell.

Deo, we're almost there.

Nothing but more images of oil-slicked creatures screeching and writhing every way he looked. Oh, crap. What the hell was that?

Without warning, her body jerked forward, her hands biting into the dragon's scales.

As they landed, Aisha followed the lead of the other women. Sliding off and stepping away.

Maddie's mouth moved furiously, and she didn't understand why at first. But she grabbed Aisha's hand and began to pull.

In front of them were five very large and very pissed off men, or rather something between human and dragon.

They stopped, though, and Maddie flashed a look to Kal. A pang of jealousy hitting Aisha as she watched the exchange. She wanted Deo to look at her that way. A look of sheer respect and understanding.

Aisha was being dragged along and almost tripped as her eyesight flickered between normal and something else.

"Careful. Also, don't let go of my hand. I've tethered our powers together," said Maddie.

Okay. What did that mean?

Blinking, Aisha suddenly saw her eyes flicker between how she normally saw things to something very different again.

Whispering to the side, she asked, "What exactly am I seeing?"

Lilly smiled.

"Maddie and I have figured out that both of us have ways to see demons through magic. I doubt either of our dad's thought about that."

Okay. Aisha would tell them they were crazy, but she was seeing this. Or seeing something. Also, this was the first time that anyone had made her feel like they saw her for what she was. A witch. A magical human, and they didn't see her as useless.

"Am I helping?"

Maddie gave a half smile as they stopped at a metal door that presumably led into the building from the rooftop.

"Yes. Things have constantly gone wrong lately. We need all the magic we can get and you, Aisha, have a lot of untapped power. Also, if you stop and feel, you should be able to sense Deo. We need you to lead us to him. Now ladies, let's pull up our big girl panties and go kick some demon ass," Maddie said.

Lilly held a hand up to the door handle. The door wasn't budging, but maybe they hadn't expected it to? Lilly's hand glowed brighter and brighter until Aisha had to look away.

She lost focus of what was going on around her as her vision shifted between the normal and this demon sight.

With her eyes closed though, Deo's thoughts flashed through her head and she finally understood what he saw. Darkness swirled. Walls moved. Her senses jumbled, but only because she tried to see things the way a human would.

Deo?

It was him. The question was, would he answer her? He was alive, but she could sense him growing weaker. What exactly was he fighting? Nothing made sense, not as she was seeing it.

"Come on," Maddie said, pulling Aisha along.

"What direction?" asked one dragon.

A moment passed until she realized all eyes were on her.

Aisha? I can sense you. Is it really you?

She locked onto his voice, using something new within her to understand where he was inside. Where was he?

It's really me. Where are you?

There was nothing for a few seconds, but she focused on the energy from him.

"Down. He's somewhere beneath us. I can't tell exactly. There's something down there."

A bright light lit up next to her and she turned to see Lilly glowing like a lantern.

"What, what is she doing?"

Maddie shrugged. "Dunno. But it's probably what she was designed to do. Let's go."

What the? Okay. Fine, she would follow, why? Because Deo was her life and he was in danger.

There was no quick descent into the bowels of the unknown. Carefully navigating the rusted stairwell, they made it down. Lilly led the way with everyone following. For being the shy, quiet one back at the ship, she seemed fearless. Aisha almost envied her confidence and her ability to be useful.

Pausing at the door marked with a large two on it, she studied the rust and chipped paint spotted metal.

"Wave your finger and do that thing you do," said Maddie.

Turning her attention away from the door, she realized Maddie was talking to her.

"What?"

Shaking her head, she shook their connected hands.

"That thing you can do with memories. Do that, but project it on the other side of the door. Do you need a memory, or can you pick up some residual from this building?"

Shrugging she held up her free hand and envisioned the same spell she'd done earlier waving her hand around the space and then as instinct took over, she pushed her palm out as if directing the spell where to go.

"Did it work?" some male asked. She didn't know who.

Deo. Hold on. We are coming for you.

She could feel his strength shifting, his mental clarity going in and out. But he was there.

Stay away. This place is crawling with demons.

She looked at her little entourage. This was the first time she wasn't alone. She'd always been alone, resilient is what she'd called herself. Her father was always there, but never understanding. Friends, though. Had she ever trusted anyone enough to call them a friend? Seconds passed before anyone moved. Even in this moment, she felt some relief.

Yeah. I think we knew that. We're coming, Deo.

Aisha trusted them and closing her own eyes, she trusted her own magic for once. Threads of power called to her on the other side of the door. She couldn't see everything, not entirely, but she could feel that it was there, intact and looping. A memory from the building in another life. Memories left trace energies everywhere, and it was just now she could see them. Memories of bad things, good things, and the mundane. She'd channeled something dark though from what she could tell. Hope that's what they wanted.

"It's working. I mean, I found trace energy from something violent. So be ready."

Maddie squeezed her hand. "It's a distraction. Perhaps the darker the better. Can you feel the dark energies on the other side of this door?"

Aisha nodded as her skin prickled and the hair on the back of her neck seemed to stand up.

Lilly did the strange light thing again against the door before. Only as the door creaked on its hinges was Aisha sure it was safe to look again.

Blinking several times, Aisha tried to wrap her head around what she was seeing. Creatures, some shapeless, others nearly human looking. One spun around and hissed, the eye sockets a soulless black. No. Not human at all.

Aisha looked at where a group of entities had gathered, and in the center played the show she'd projected. She looked away as the realization she'd conjured up looked like a murder.

The good thing was it indeed distracted a hoard of demons.

"Will they attack us?"

Aisha caught Maddie's eyes.

"This is Lilly's domain, not mine."

A shiver chased up her spine, and she bit back the acidic burn coming up her throat.

Something dark, with a long tongue-looking thing appeared out of nowhere and hovered in front of her. She gasped and nearly screamed, except she was paralyzed. She couldn't scream. She wanted to. Nothing would come out. Her eyes widened as the tongue lashed out, but instead of reaching her skin, it began to burn, and a horrible screeching filled the space. She tried to drop Maddie's hand to cover her ears but couldn't.

"You can't let go. The spell won't let you. The blood running through Lilly is the strongest defense we have. You don't want to let go."

It was then that she took a quick look around and realized that they weren't being followed. Or well, they were, but not by the dragons.

"Where, where are your mates?"

Maddie shook her head. "I couldn't tether Kal to me and realized the magic wouldn't work on them. They are here for backup. Now, tell us which direction is Deo in?"

Aisha opened her mind, moving past the fact she'd nearly

been a demon's lunch. A few seconds in and she could feel his heartbeat.

"This way," she said, and took off pulling the other two with her. Her eyes tried to play tricks on her, but she could see through the illusions the demons projected. She went straight where dead ends appeared and turned when the building disappeared. Until they cleared the last obstacle and saw a massive figure lying down. A dragon. He lay in the middle of the floor. His eyes nearly white.

Deo? Deo, answer me.

She watched for a sign of anything, until finally he blinked.

I'm here, my mate. I am here.

Aisha tried to run faster, but the dead weight of the other two slowed her.

Fine. Whatever.

They were almost there. She could almost touch him. She almost had him back, safe, where she could tell him she wanted him. No amount of money could replace what she had.

Looking over her shoulder she nearly screamed at the two women, but why were they moving so slowly, stopping as the other two women came to a halt.

What is that? she asked Deo instinctually. He always had the answer.

The large beast started to rise on hind legs, multiple legs from what Aisha could see. Yeah. This wasn't normal.

She spoke out of the side of her mouth. "What do we do with that?"

No one said anything.

"Uh, I don't know. Can you ask Deo if he can carry us, with you guiding him through your shared connection?"

Aisha wanted to panic but pushed the bubble of terror down. For now.

Deo? Can you carry us?

She didn't dare turn around, but a moment later his muzzle was against her palm.

Yes. As long as you are with me, I can do anything.

Her head slowly bobbed as Lilly slid back, pulling the other two with her.

Once they were next to Deo, they worked as a team to get on, except well they stopped at the sight of a woman.

Maddie and Lilly flashed a look to Aisha, but what the hell was she going to say.

"Just get on," she yelled.

Maddie nearly slid off, but Aisha and Lilly pulled her up

Go.

Aisha didn't really understand what she was doing until she did it. She guided Deo through the maze of illusions with something large snarling and growling at their heels.

I can't fight it, he said to her.

There was nothing to say back. She didn't want him to fight that. She wanted to be outside on the roof top away from whatever the hell that was.

She would need a few days at the very least to process what the hell just happened.

One more turn, she shared with him the last hall and he sped up.

Lilly screamed from the back as they neared the doorway. "Close your eyes."

Aisha did as told, and now they were running blind into a stairwell that Deo wasn't going to fit through as a dragon.

Shit.

Jump, he yelled into her head and she scanned it to the others.

As she did, Deo shifted, the unconscious woman dropping to the ground, and then Aisha dragged Maddie and Lilly into the hall only to lose Lilly as they dove through the door.

She closed her eyes as a bright white light shot out like lightning into the room.

"Climb," Deo yelled.

"Lilly?" Aisha yelled, peeking against her better judgment.

Deo grabbed her and carried her over his shoulder as she suddenly saw Kal drop from the stairs above to grab Maddie and lastly Eadric skipping every stair on the way down.

Eadric will have her.

Aisha covered her ears as millions of screams rang out into the air. No reprieve came even on the roof. The only thing she could think was that it sounded like a million souls being burned alive.

Just as quickly as it started, the world went silent and Deo dropped to the tarred surface.

He gently put Aisha down before he collapsed.

"Deo? Deo, answer me."

Nothing.

She tried again.

Deo? Don't you die on me now.

No. This wasn't happening. She'd just gotten him back. He couldn't die. He couldn't leave her.

"Don't leave me. I can't live without you." She pounded on his shoulder, but nothing happened.

I love you. I need to tell you that. To tell you that I never traded you for money. I need to tell you I need you.

Nothing.

Aisha didn't bother to notice who grabbed at her. Let a demon take her. She was numb. She'd been here before.

No. This was worse. So much worse.

She couldn't even cry.

eo grabbed his side as he attempted to sit up. That was going to leave a mark.

"Brother, it's good to see those beautiful blue eyes of yours," said Cy.

"Shit. You're the one that saved me? Goddess, did you leave everything intact?"

His brother chuckled. "Ah, there are just some things, even I can't fix. Like that sense of humor and the size of -"

"Deo," Aisha screamed and nearly jumped into his lap.

He let out a woosh of air as she hit his side.

"Oh, I'm so sorry," she said, pulling away and looking at the bandages.

Cy rolled his eyes behind her. "If one more hard-headed female joins this bunch, I'm getting a transfer far, far away."

Deo laughed with Cy.

"Call if you need anything brother," Cy said, as he left.

Deo heard him but was much too focused on his Aisha.

"I am fine, mate."

He stroked her hair as she clung to his neck.

"I thought I lost you," she said, a sob in her voice.

A few things he did know, one being how fucking amazing it was just to hold her again.

"I'm so sorry. I never traded you, or sold you, or whatever that guy said. He offered-"

"It's okay, mate. I know." He ran his hands up and down her back, loving every inch of her. He never wanted to be away from her again. There was nothing worse, and he truly understood this now. All other pain in the world couldn't compare to thinking you'd lost your soulmate.

"You know?"

Pulling away, she sat up, the motion rubbing more than just some sensitive scrapes.

"Yes. At first, I didn't. I believe fear demons may have been a part of it, but once I realized that I still wasn't free to mate with another female, I knew that you hadn't rejected me. I realized the emptiness I felt wasn't that of rejection, but -"

She stopped him with a finger. Deo kissed the digit against his lips.

"Wait. Wait. Just wait. Mate with another female?"

His mouth quirked as visions filtered from her mind to him. What was the word he needed right now? Jealousy?

"Yes, my love. Mate. I was never meant to remain there, I was only requested to give my seed to another female. But I could not," he said, watching her ears start to burn red.

Funny little mate.

"Just? You were just supposed to screw some woman? And then they would let you go?"

He eyed her. The images in her head confusing.

"Yes," caution lacing his words. She grabbed his face between her hands.

"Then why didn't you? You could have been back with me sooner? Without being injured."

Deo studied her. Was she serious? This was not expected.

Mated females were no more likely to share than their males would. He would have killed anyone who touched her.

"You would have me believe that it would not have bothered you if I had just screwed, as you called it, another female?"

She slapped his shoulder. Lucky for him it wasn't hurt.

She was small in stature, curvy in all the right places, and damn if she wasn't stronger than he gave her credit for.

"No, you ass. Of course I'd hate you. But," she said, a frown forming and her eyes dimming.

Deo tried to read her thoughts.

Mate? Why do you frown?

He watched as a small droplet of water escaped her eyes. Brushing it away with a finger, he waited patiently for her. He thought sharing a connection would help him understand her, but he was wrong. Or he was wrong so far.

I want all of you; I don't want to share you. And now that I know who the other woman is, well, it just sucks.

Deo adjusted himself on the bed in their infirmary. He wanted to get back to their room and kiss away the sadness.

"Mate. I could not leave her. It would not be right. Besides, as soon as she is healthy she will be taken back to her home."

As he breathed Aisha's scent in, his need for her grew. He'd been starved of his new mate for too long. Hours? A day? He really wasn't sure. That place had been a labyrinth and time didn't exist.

Deo had tried to remember everything that had happened, but it was disjointed in his own mind. He'd been in and out of sleep for a few hours, but he didn't want to talk to anyone. He didn't think he could fully comprehend what had happened.

Fucking demons. He'd been prepared to handle the consequences. He'd been able to use instinct to get him as far as they had, but that last creature. Well, he still wasn't sure what it was as it had clawed his human body. He'd shifted much too late that time, and Deo blamed the demon energy.

Seeing her sadness, feeling it, he knew he shouldn't mention that saving the female had been the biggest risk.

Aisha still hadn't spoken. He tried to focus on her scent and controlling his need for her as the seconds ticked by. How could he make her see that his love for her had never been in question? From the moment he saw her, he knew she was meant to be his.

"Aisha, that woman never had a chance, but she also didn't deserve to die either."

She nodded, it was at least some sign of life.

"Yeah. I know. I'm mad at myself. If you would have, you know, done that, it would have been my fault. I should have told you about creepy scientist guy sooner. Reality is, I was pretty much so desperate to tell you how I felt that I forgot about everything else. It's like I was a love-struck teenager again."

That made little sense to him, but the sentiment wasn't lost on him either.

"Well, I appreciate that you did. I was growing less and less an honorable mate every time I saw you." He gripped her hips, ignoring the burning in his side. It would heal. The ache between his legs, on the other hand, wasn't going away. Not with her this close. The scent of her tantalizing him.

He smirked as he watched her eyes grow a little wider. "Don't worry, mate. I would have ensured you said yes before I mated you properly, but I was growing more and more desperate. You are the most enticing female I have ever seen."

A blush peeked out from under her shirt and climbed her neck. He enjoyed being able to make her squirm.

Leaning in, his mouth an inch from her ear, he whispered, "I wanted to taste you from the moment I laid eyes on you."

Dipping his head, he kissed the crook of her neck. She shivered under his hands.

"I want to taste you now," he continued to say.

Aisha couldn't hide her thoughts from him, and a smile spread over his lips.

"But you're hurt," she said.

Yes, but that's not what you are thinking.

She gasped.

Out of my head.

He pulled her closer.

I like the thoughts running through your mind.

Kissing along the pulse in her neck, along her jaw, he waited for her to turn her lips to his. Her thoughts were having a hard time arguing.

But, your side.

She pulled away and studied him. He didn't like it when she scrutinized the situation. He knew this look and knew it would be a fight.

He slid his hand around her neck, pulling her closer. Perhaps if he distracted her long enough.

"I don't want to hurt you, Deo," she said.

Absently, he wrapped his fingers in her hair as he locked his gaze with hers.

"I welcome the pain of knowing I am alive, here, with you. You still don't understand that you not only bring my soul peace, you strengthen me."

She tilted her head. Her words said one thing, but her thought said she enjoyed the sensations of his fingers against her neck.

"So, by strengthening you, do you mean you might heal faster closer to me?"

Deo licked his lips. Trailing a finger over the neckline of her shirt, he shrugged.

"Should we test out this theory?" he asked.

His eye caught the marking, peeking under her shirt on her shoulder. His hand traced over the fabric where the start of his markings on her skin peeked out under the tank top.

She moaned.

Deo realized that he had yet to have the chance to explore his new mate as any dragon should. He didn't know how his markings appeared on her. Would they be as large? Would they cover her beautiful breasts? The idea of seeing them only made his dick harder. He shifted her on his lap to give himself more room.

Pulling aside the strap of the shirt, he began to kiss the swirling design unique to him and his mate. The intricate lines started to glow the blue of his dragon's power as his lips connected with each piece.

She moaned.

Aisha tilted her head away, stretching her neck to give him more access as he followed the path under the neckline. Hooking a finger, he pulled the stretchy fabric further and growled as the design scrawled lower, stopping above her breast similar to his own, although he enjoyed hers more.

His fingers itched to touch, and he no longer cared about her protests. He needed her.

A long claw came out of his hand as he ripped through the fabric. His dragon would not allow her to refuse them again either. She was theirs. He would never be denied again.

"Deo, what the hell."

He mumbled against her neck. "You have more of these annoying clothes, and I need you now."

Flashes of her on top made it hard for him to think any further. The weight between his legs making logic impossible.

Cupping her breasts, he licked at the skin of her shoulder before dipping his head to take the now taught peak into his mouth. Her hands tangled with his hair as the scent of her arousal filled the air.

"Deo, we aren't alone."

He flashed images of his mouth swallowing her screams of pleasure as she rode him. Deo didn't really care. His brothers would stay away.

We are alone enough. No one will bother us.

Her face flushed an adorable pink again. He liked when she flushed for far better reasons.

We can go back to our room if you prefer.

Aisha glared. "Are you even allowed to?"

Rolling his eyes, he pushed his pelvis up against her bottom.

I am well, and I don't care. Simple scratches. I just want you.

Before he said anything else, she leaned in and started kissing him this time. He needed her. He needed to feel whole again, and she was the missing ingredient.

Yes. Scratches, she thought.

A quick glance and he saw her eyes were half lidded. Good. He was getting to her. He was done waiting.

Sliding a hand to her lower back, he pulled her closer. She didn't need coaxing as she began to rub against the bulge under the sheet.

Pulling away, she broke the kiss.

"Fine, but I'm doing all the work to make sure you don't hurt that," she said and pointed to his bandage.

Whatever you say, mate.

It was then, as he slid his hand up her thigh, that he found out she was wearing a skirt. He groaned and slid his fingers down the edge of her panties.

He cupped her heat over the fabric and smiled against her mouth as he felt the cotton dampen. He hooked a finger in the fabric and pulled it aside. Running his finger over the bare skin of her lips, she squirmed.

Aisha gripped at the sheet covering him and pulled it down. She lifted herself and slid it even further down his legs.

"I can't wait any longer," she said, raising her hips over his dick as he held her panties aside.

He held his breath at the pleasure of her seating herself on his shaft. She slowly stretched her muscles around him, lifting herself up, and then pushing back down, taking more of him in. He tore her tank top off completely this time and gripped her breasts as she began to ride him, rocking her hips.

Her mouth hungry against his as she began a fevered pace of

want and need. He thrust against her, giving her more contact, driving his shaft deeper. This time, in her head, he could read her thoughts as she grew closer and closer to release.

He could feel her need for him. She wrapped her arms around his neck, pulling herself as close to him as she could.

She was so close, and he would finish her even if he couldn't flip her over and take her the way he wanted. Instead, he slipped his finger over her clit and stroked her as she pushed forward, her hips rocking faster and faster.

She called his name as her body quivered around him, and the pressure of her release was just enough to pull his own from him.

Kissing her lips, her neck, the mark on her shoulder, Deo held her. Nothing made sense in this world without her.

His dragon breathed a sigh, finally contented. Yes, he could take on anything with her by his side.

*A*isha glared at Maddie.

"That wasn't helpful," she said, staring down at a now live fly.

Maddie smiled. "You just said you wanted to know how to heal someone. Well, the fly was still twitching, therefore healable. It wouldn't work if the person was dead, or if there were extensive life-threatening injuries."

Aisha sighed. This was helpful. It really was. But it wasn't something she could give to human doctors. Not yet.

"Thanks, Maddie. Now I can put on my resume that I can heal flies. I'm sure the medical community is going to be so happy. All we needed were more flies."

Maddie threw her hands up. "Hey, you asked, and I showed you. Tell you what, if you can find a nearly dead lizard out here in the desert, I can show you how to heal it?"

They both laughed. At least this was passing the time, for now.

Lilly walked in flanked by Eadric.

Kal and Deo walked in after them, and Aisha jumped out of her seat.

"I'm so glad you're back," she said, wrapping her arms around his neck.

Calm yourself.

Although he sounded so casual, he planted a kiss on her that said he'd missed her just as much.

How is your wing? Okay?

He nodded. *It is getting there. Thank you for the salve.*

Aisha blushed. For the first time, she felt useful and not just for healing a fly. She'd actually been able to use her knowledge and some of Lilly's magic. She came up with a special balm for Deo that could heal his demon inflicted wounds. For the first time in days, he'd been able to fly. They'd left one brother behind to keep watch out for the ship, while the rest flanked Deo to ensure he didn't drop like a rock out of the sky. Their words, not Aisha's. She'd hated the term and almost hadn't let him go.

"Are you ready to go back to the room?" she asked.

Mate, I'm supposed to be healing.

Aisha gave him a poke in the ribs. *That wasn't what I was implying, but since you brought it up.*

"We will be back shortly." Deo wrapped her in his arms and carried her back to their room.

As the door closed behind them, Aisha kissed down his chest, never tiring of his hard muscles. As she rounded his side, she saw the nasty scar that had struggled to heal.

"Did you guys talk about that asshole doctor yet? And the Illuminati group? I mean, we aren't leaving until your brothers find their mates, right?"

Deo nodded. "Yeah. We think it's time to find Lilly's sister. But right now, let's not worry about that. Lay down and spread your legs for me."

Can't wait for more dragons? Get sneak peeks early! Sign up for my newsletter www.michellezieglerauthor.com/contact!

Space Dragons Seek Mates
Book 1: Must Love Dragons
Book 2: Single Red Dragon
Book 2.5 Dragons Under the Mistletoe
Book 3: Dragon Wanted
COMING SOON!
Book 4: Looking for a Good Dragon
She's caught between his rock-solid body and a hard place.

Book 5: No Scales Needed
Book 6: Desperately Seeking Dragon

Do you like fate? Or maybe you're tired of waiting for it. Try Michelle's

<u>Move Over Fate Series</u>

When it Raines, He Purrs

Icing on His Mate

Snowy with a Chance of Mating

ABOUT THE AUTHOR

Michelle's imagination started spilling out onto paper the second she could scribble. Her drawing never improved, but her love affair with words continued and evolved as she became infatuated with one story after another. If life could be written, Michelle would write everyone's ending as a happily ever after.

Michelle grew up in Chicago and later moved to Colorado. Her husband still makes fun of her Midwest accent. She has traded in her engineering degree to raise two little humans and three dogs, and prays she survives it all. Her sanity survives on the pages she writes. As Michelle always says, in a world of serious she writes an escape.

Website: http://www.michelleziegerauthor.com
Newsletter: http://michelleziegerauthor.com/contact/

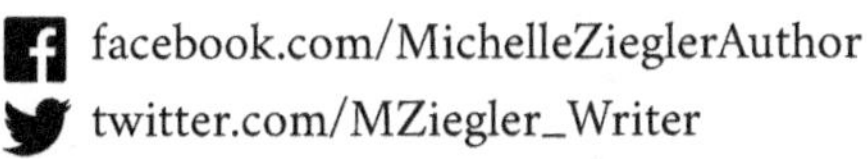

facebook.com/MichelleZieglerAuthor
twitter.com/MZiegler_Writer
instagram.com/mziegler_writer

www.ingramcontent.com/pod-product-compliance
Lightning Source LLC
Chambersburg PA
CBHW071619150726

48000CB00004B/1787